Climbing Mount Fuji

And other tales of a teenager in Japan
During the 1950's

By

Orlando Stephenson

Introduction

From 1955 to 1958 my dad, who was a Lieutenant Colonel in the United States Air Force, was stationed in Japan. We lived at Johnson Air Force Base in Irumagawa, Japan, a prefecture about an hour north of Tokyo. This book is a collection of memories from the three years I spent there, my first three years of high school.

They are all mostly true stories or, at least, as true as my mind can remember some fifty years later. Some are very clear and to the point, some have morals, some are to illustrate a point, and some are just those crystal-clear crackling sledge hammer moments that punctuate all of our lives. Those few moments that jump up and bite us hard and are burned into our memories.

Those moments that separate the normal day to day grind. Those of us who got to live there got a lot of those moments in Japan.

It was a magical time.

Those dependents who were lucky enough to have been stationed in Japan during the 50's, 60's or 70's know what I mean. As teenagers we were treated like adults. We had almost no boundaries. We could go anywhere and do almost anything that adults could do. It colored our upbringing and made it much richer and a lot more fun.

A lot of responsibility came with this lack of boundaries and sometimes, since we were kids, we didn't handle it properly, well, sometimes we handled it very badly.

I had some of those "handle it badly times" but they too became part of the fondness that I have of my teenage years in Japan. I hope that this book is clear enough to convey to you what it was like.

Table of Contents

Forward

I want to talk about the word 'well'.

I use the word well a lot in this book.

I know it is probably not correct, or at least not acceptable to use well all the time like I do.

An editor will probably hate it.

I use it when I have an epiphany, or to make a point, to punctuate, to present a new thought, a new view, an inspiration, or when I want to change the direction of the story. I probably should use something more artful, but well works for me.

Well, I hope you understand.

Orlando

p.s. All the kids in my family were called by their middle names, thus I appear as Worth in this book. How I came to be called Orlando (my first name) is another story.

Edwin D. Patrick

Our trip to Japan in 1955 was by boat. Actually, I guess something that big is known as a ship. Our ship was the General Edwin D. Patrick (originally named the Admiral C.F. Hughes), a troop ship during the war that had been converted into a luxury liner for ferrying dependent families to Japan.

Perhaps luxury liner is a bit of a stretch as it didn't have those modern-day necessities that many cruise ships have now such as an eighteen-hole golf course, or climbing walls, or a white water kayak course, or an ice rink, or hang gliding but, it did have shuffleboard, ping pong, tennis, a ballroom and lots of food. At fourteen I thought this was a luxury liner.

Our transfer to Japan started in the summer of 1955 when Mom and us five kids left New Orleans (our semi-permanent home at the time that we had returned to while Dad was in Korea) and flew to San Francisco to settle down with all the other dependent families slated for the Edwin D. at the Presidio. We waited three days while it returned from Japan, offloaded cargo and dependent families coming home and got ready for us.

We had barely backed out of the slip when the lifeboat drill started, my first ever and, as such, a novelty. We, of course, received all the dire warnings of how important it was to show up, how in a real emergency you could die without this practice, and, more importantly, how you would be punished (like maybe being dragged behind the ship, or even keel-hauled) for failure to appear.

All the same warnings I have heard countless times since. Warnings that just mean that you and almost all the other passengers stand at your lifeboat station in the hot sun, or freezing cold, or rain, or whatever, longer than you should have to, while they try to find those inconsiderate, thoughtless, selfish, or perhaps deaf or brain-dead passengers who had no intention of participating. Those same passengers whom I have never, ever, seen being dragged behind the ship or keel-hauled later.

During this drill, we passed Alcatraz and then steamed right under the Golden

Gate, with the sun setting just in front of us. Wow, our adventure had begun. It was scary and exciting at the same time. As a military brat I had, of course, changed homes many times but this was more than just being stationed in Albuquerque or Great Falls, or Knob Noster, Missouri. We were leaving the country, headed for a foreign place. Would I love or it hate it, would I fit in, what about the language, what about...?

The list is endless, it is a list that as dependents we dealt with about every three years as we moved like gypsies to a new place. This time, however, felt different. It felt like it was going to be more exciting, mysterious and challenging. Little did I realize at the time just how memorable the next three years would be.

This trip marked the beginning of the unparalleled freedom and lack of adult supervision that I was to enjoy for the next three years. I didn't know it at the time but, in effect, I had just become an adult at fourteen. Maybe not really truely an adult but in many, no, in most ways I began my adulthood. A screwed up, immature, juvenile, inexperienced, naive kind of an adult but an adult, nevertheless.

Wait, that last sentence sounds like a lot of "adults" I know today.

The reason I started out on this trip with very little supervision is related to the way the military and military wives function socially. The military has a reflected caste system when it comes to wives. The wife of the highest-ranking person becomes, by that and that alone, the leader of all the other wives.

My mother, as the wife of a Lt Col, was the "highest ranking wife" on the vessel. As such she was responsible for "leading" the other wives, which meant that she was quite busy planning parties, bridge tournaments, shuffleboard contests, and other events to occupy the nine days that we would be at sea. My brother, who was thirteen, and I were free to do whatever we wanted. I think mom figured that we were confined to a ship so how far could we go, and how much trouble could we possibly get into.

Pretty far as it turned out. As I said there weren't any of the incredible number of things to do that are available on modern day cruise ships, so we rapidly got bored. Ping-pong and shuffleboard just weren't going to keep us occupied for the long days, there was only one cute girl our age who wasn't interested and meals only used up about three hours.

If you've ever taken a trans-oceanic voyage you know what I mean. Without something to keep you entertained you eat but, you can only eat so much. Then you start looking around. Then you see those signs that say, "crew only." Those signs become challenges for the bored, or, intellectually challenged.

Actually, in our culture we respect those signs, because they work, unless you are young savages, like we had just become, with no one to keep us in check. We found out that below decks there was another world.

The passengers lived on the decks that were above water, decks six, seven, and eight. Below that on decks three, four, and five there were bunks for 5000 troops! Down a couple of decks from where we had cabins, past those "crew only" signs and there you were, looking down row after row of canvas bunks, four high, that stretched on forever.

Your heart beat fast because of the forbidden place you were in and because you could feel the masses of humanity who had to have lived here, even if but for a short time, worrying about where they were going, worrying if they were going to sink and die from a sub, dreaming about their wives, girlfriends, moms and dads.

It was horrible. I know it was a necessary horrible but to this day I have a picture of those bunks in my mind and I grieve for the reasons that made living like that necessary.

About halfway into the trip we crossed the international date line, originally a rite of passage for sailors their first-time crossing, it was used as an excuse to consume an entire day with ceremony and fooling around.

All the passengers and crew who hadn't crossed the line before were deemed Pollywogs. We were made to dress up with our clothing on backward, we were taken through various obstacles, including going down to the lowest deck of the ship, right in the bow (a place my brother and I hadn't gotten to yet) where we had to crawl on our hands and knees, had raw eggs cracked on our heads, and otherwise made fun of while "King Neptune" (ruler of the high seas) and his trusty court looked on.

At the end of the day we were made to kneel in front of "King Neptune" and swear our loyalty. This transformed us from Pollywogs to Shellbacks and we each received a certificate. It passed a day.

Arrival

The birds had been the first clue that we were close. For two days now there had been birds circling and landing on the ship. Especially the seagulls, who went crazy when the crew threw the meal scraps and other garbage overboard. The captain had made an announcement that we'd make landfall today and this was visual proof that we were close. We were excited and scared. A move to a new station was always uncomfortable but this was a strange land as well.

"Look, Worth," my brother shouted. "I see it!"

"I looked where he was pointing and didn't see anything but the clean gray line that we had been looking at for over a week.

"Baird," I chided, "it's just your imagination."

"No, Worth," he insisted, "look!"

I looked again and still didn't see anything. I was about to turn away when something caught my eye. I blinked and... sure enough there was a little smudge on the horizon.

"You might be right," I said, carefully. "I think I see something."

We stood at the rail for over an hour with our eyes glued to that smudge. While we watched, it gradually lifted itself out of the ocean and became land. We were there!

Well, we were there was a bit of a misnomer as, it took hours before we entered Tokyo bay and steamed up to the port of Yokohama. Then another eternity while the tug boats pushed and pulled our ship, the U.S.S. Edwin D. Patrick, into position at the pier and we tied up.

Unlike our departure from San Francisco, nine days before, when the pier had been empty, this one was a teeming mass of humanity. Dozens of porters, immigration officials, geisha girls and U.S. Military forces milled about while the obligatory Military band played rousing Sousa marches.

"Look, Worth," Baird shouted, pointing to where they were rolling out the gangplank, "there's dad."

I followed his finger and sure enough our dad had managed to talk his way past the immigration officers, probably because of his rank, and was waiting patiently to come aboard. Dressed in kakis with his soft dress hat perched to one side of his head he looked happy and relaxed. We waved and hollered, but with the din he couldn't hear us.

"Let's go back to mom's cabin," I said, "he'll go there first."

In the main cabin that mom had shared with our youngest brother and sister our mother was watching our room steward haul the four steamer trunks she had packed with the household goods we brought with us out into the passageway. I ducked into the cabin that Baird and I and our middle brother Gene shared across the hall and pulled our suitcases into the passageway.

"We saw dad, mom," Baird gushed, "he looks great!"

"And it looks like they're letting him come on board," I added.

Her face flushed and she immediately turned to the mirror. I looked at her fussing with her hair and putting on lipstick and realized that my mom was probably a very attractive woman (considering how old she looked to me) and was clearly looking forward as much as we were to seeing dad.

Then, as if she had some sixth sense, she stopped what she was doing and turned to the door. Dad stuck his head around the corner a second later. Baird and I started to rush for a hug, but mom beat us to him. He swept her into his arms and crushed her lips against his while Baird and I and our three other siblings waited patiently and with tinges of embarrassment.

Finally, they broke their embrace and looked at us. We all clambered to get our hug. Dad embraced and looked at each of us in turn and then reached down and scooped up Marc, our youngest brother, in his right arm, gathered our mother in his left and grinned at us. It had been a long year while he had been stationed in Korea but now, we were a family again.

Dad looked at Baird and me and asked, "You boys ready to head to your new home?"

Neither of us dared to speak. We were ready but we knew nothing about this country and were feeling overwhelmed. I nodded and Baird followed suit.

"Let's go then," he said, "We've got a long trip."

He strode off down the passageway with mom on one arm and Marc on the other while the rest of us trailed along like baby ducklings or perhaps more like children following the pied piper of Hameln to an unknown and uncertain fate.

By the time we got off the ship and onto the pier it was packed with our fellow travelers standing in long lines to pass through immigration and customs. Dad paid the lines no attention but rather stepped to a barrier on the end and motioned to a Japanese official. Two minutes later we were past all the formalities and out in the parking lot being escorted to a blue Air Force bus by the driver and trailed by six Japanese porters toting our luggage. The porters put the luggage in, we piled in and we were off.

What I saw out the window as we drove through the Yokohama Naval Base was soothing. I could have been anywhere. Anywhere or everywhere in the world that is, where the American military have created their own little communities that are homes away from home. Wide streets, beautifully manicured lawns, men in uniform and women in poodle skirts walking dogs, it was a scene I had been part of many times in my short life.

Then we passed through the main gate into the city of Yokohama and my world changed forever. The tastefully sculpted spaces gave way to wall-to-wall bars on both sides of the street whose sole purpose was to cater to the thousands of sailors stationed there, giving them the least possible quantity of products and services for the maximum amount of lightening of their wallets that they could achieve.

Everywhere I looked there were teeming masses of humanity on bicycles, walking, riding in three wheelers, streetcars, busses, honey wagons and very old American cars. The streets had become narrow, congested and winding and all the street signs and shop signs were in strange symbols that were and would for the most part remain totally indecipherable to me for my entire time in Japan.

It was overwhelming and very frightening. I suddenly felt lost and I remember thinking that I couldn't do this. I glanced at my father, but he was deep into conversation with my mom. I looked out of the window again and the trepidation of my situation threatened to consume me.

That moment was and remains one of the signal moments of my life. When you think about it you have memories, and then you have MEMORIES. You have thousands of memories of things that you have done, both good and bad, softly lying in your mind keeping you company, causing you to nod your head when they flit through your brain. They are things that you remember that give you a warm sensation or sometimes a squirrelly uncomfortable one.

Along with that you also have a few MEMORIES, those signal, sometimes life-changing, sometimes bittersweet, sometimes no real reason to remember moments that are as fresh in your mind as if they had happened an hour ago.

Like that time that your wife was in labor and the doctor wasn't there, and he walked in just as the baby was halfway out. No time to scrub, no time to put on a gown, he just rolled up his sleeves, stuck out his arms and your son was in his hands. That kind of MEMORY.

For some reason that moment in my life is forever in my mind. We were driving on a street with thousands of people and hundreds of unreadable signs and my world and my mind closed down and I was completely lost.

But I was fourteen and that lost feeling passed in the flicker of a fourteen-year old's attention span and I soon became engrossed in the new sights and sounds and smells of my new home, Japan in the late 1950's.

Johnson Air Force Base, where my father was stationed was about an hour and a half drive from Yokohama. It had been a Japanese air base during the war called Irumagawa Air Base and had been one of the major staging points for the much-feared Kamikaze suicide planes that wreaked havoc on our fleet.

As we entered the main gate the world transformed itself again into a copy of anywhere USA. Wide straight streets, traffic but no congestion, and a total lack of the masses of humanity that we had been passing for the past hour and a half. It was paradise. At least it was a paradise for those of us who were used to burgers, fries and American pie. There was a movie theater, barber shop, teen club, BX, Commissary, mini-mart, football field, officer's club, three pools and a burger stand.

I relaxed again. I could do this. It was almost like...

Oops, all of a sudden we went out of the other side of the base and chaos returned.

"Dad," I asked, "Where are we going?"

"Home, Worth," he said.

"But, dad, the base is back there," I said pointing to the gate that was receding behind us.

.

"There isn't any base housing available for us yet," he said.

"What?"

"We are going to live off base," he explained.

"Off base?"

"I rented us a Japanese house," he said.

I looked at the shacks that were scrolling by the window. Japanese houses looked... well they certainly didn't look like anything I wanted to live in. I must have whimpered my displeasure because he laughed and tousled my hair.

"Trust me son," he said, "you are going to love our new home."

I didn't answer. I stared out of the window glumly wondering how I was going to survive the next three years as the scenery got worse. We turned into a dirt road that wound its way up a hill. Halfway up we turned into a gravel parking area in front of what looked like the entrance to a Japanese shrine. Three Japanese women in Kimono were standing on the steps.

"This is it, boys," dad said, bounding out of the bus.

I looked again and it still looked like a temple to me. I followed the rest of them out of the bus and stood looking up at the three women on the steps. Two of them were average Japanese women that even in the few hours that I had been in this country I had seen numerous examples of. Short and stocky with darker skin and flat faces with big smiles. Their names (as I learned later) were Sumiko and Yoshiko. They were dressed in kimono and bowing deeply to greet us. They greeted us with 'Ohiyogosaimasu', Japanese for good morning or good day, our first words in a new land. Those three women would remain with us for our entire three years in Japan,

The woman on the left was an exception. She was pretty with high cheekbones, a slender nose and a startlingly clear complexion. Only her eyes gave away that she was Japanese. As my dad approached, she bowed deeply and said, "Konichiwa, Ojii-san" (Good afternoon, grandfather).

He bowed back and said, "Konichiwa, Nobuko."

My father had always been the type to really immerse himself in whatever endeavor occupied his interest. Among other endeavors he was a gourmet cook, a square dance caller, a sailor, a gardener, a marine captain... A man of many talents and now, clearly, he had decided to learn Japanese.

We followed our parents up the steps into the entranceway and got our first taste of Japanese style living.

The house was laid out in a typical Japanese design for an upper middle-class family. Huge main entrance from the road into a courtyard for parking. Three steps up to the main entryway where there were low benches to sit on to remove your shoes and then one step up to the tatami mat covered foyer. At the back of the foyer were shoji (rice paper) screens that slid open to reveal a hall with hand polished wooden floor that ran down the back side of the house. There was one main room to the right that served as a bedroom and two to the left that also served as bedrooms but the middle one was also the living room during the day. Japanese style also means that all the floors were tatami mats with futons on the floor for bedding which was is put away during the day and each room had a low table in the middle to sit around.

The main living room also had a charcoal hibachi for the colder winter months. At the left end of the hall was a toilet cubicle and then the hall turned at an angle of about 70 degrees and went back to the kitchen, bath and two more rooms for the maids. There was a Japanese rock garden out the back and all around were trees and bushes that formed a pleasingly decorative screen from the outside world.

We lived in that home for three months until base housing became available. The experience of the house, the newness of it all, the lack of friends because school hadn't started yet, and the closeness to the local town rapidly accelerated my adaptation to the culture.

I soon found myself shopping for Zori (what we now call flip-flops, a very common form of footwear in Japan at the time and which I wore most of my time there) and playing Pachinko at one of the parlors in Irumagawa instead of heading out to the teen club or the burger joint at the base.

 We moved to base housing just as school started, when my world changed to Occidental again.

Narimasu

Our school was called Narimasu and was in Tokyo about an hour and a half drive from Johnson Air Force Base.

Narimasu is a form of the verb 'naru' in Japanese. It is the polite positive present indicative form which can mean several things but in this case the translation is 'to learn'. I never asked why or how the powers that be named the school that, but I guess it makes sense although Japanese was not offered as a course while I attended.

The reason for its location was that many dependents lived in Tokyo proper and three major Air Force Bases (Johnson, Yakota, Tachikawa) which were in an arc around Tokyo, each about the same distance away. Thus, all the dependents in Tokyo and on those bases could commute to school fairly easily.

If you hadn't known you were in Japan, you wouldn't have been able to tell by the school. It was no different than my final year of high school which I did in

Dayton, Ohio. Well, it was, but not in the superficial things. The big difference was the level of sophistication of the whole student body. A student body completely comprised of Army brats who had a leg up on kids who had never been subjected to the pressures of being forced to move every three years.

Narimasu had football, basketball, cheerleaders, a band, a yearbook, hot lunches, track, lockers, blackboards, letter sweaters, chess club, science club, and... Well, you get the idea. It was just like any high school anywhere even including our teams competing with other schools in other parts of Japan.

The beauty of an hour to an hour and a half commute was that it gave you plenty of time to do your homework on the way home or on the way in if you had procrastinated.

Of course, no school could possibly be a real copy of a Stateside school without Prom. Boy did we have Prom.

Because of the spread-out nature of the student body and because many of the other young savages enjoyed the same freedoms that I did the Narimasu Prom was never held in the gym.

Each year the Prom committee rented a ballroom in a downtown Tokyo hotel, decorated it according to that year's theme, hired a band and put on one hell of a bash. I honestly can't remember chaperones. I do remember booze.

I got lucky for my Junior Prom. About three weeks prior to Prom I was still looking for a date. Then a miracle happened. Normally because of school years, families are rotated into and out of Japan during the summer months. Once in a great while they are uprooted during the school year.

That was my miracle. Three weeks before Prom a super cute new girl got on the bus going to school. She was crying and looked lost and lonely and upset which made sense because we all felt like that every time we changed stations.

As she got to where I was sitting, I stood up and asked her to sit with me. She had only arrived the day before and knew absolutely no one so she sat.

Her name was Kitty and by the end of that ride to school I had asked her to go steady and to Prom and she had accepted.

For Prom my dad hired a driver for our 1950 Buick. I picked Kitty up at four in the afternoon and he drove us into Tokyo. I took her to dinner at a fancy restaurant (remember this was post war Japan so that meal probably cost no more than five dollars), ending up at the hotel where Prom was about 8pm. We danced, had a few drinks, visited with friends and traded lies until about ten.

Then a group of us headed out for some of the nightclubs and other places that were regular stops for us when we went into Tokyo to party. We stopped at three over the course of the next few hours, drinking, eating, dancing, having fun and oh, yes... kissing.

I fondly remember Salmenos where the ceilings were so low that I couldn't stand up straight. It had candles on the tables which everyone used to write in soot on the ceiling. They clearly had a crew to repaint the ceiling regularly as none of the clever things I wrote were there on a subsequent visit.

I got Kitty home at four in the morning. The driver cost me a thousand yen which, at the time was just under three dollars.

The coda to that lovely night was that Kitty broke up with me a few days later and hooked up with a football jock. She was way out of my league and I knew it when I approached her, but what a ride while it lasted.

I don't remember my Senior year Prom back in the States.

I know I had a date and I know I went and I'm sure it was nice but...

Contact lenses

When I was in the sixth grade, I found out that I couldn't see. Well, I didn't know I couldn't see but my parents figured it out because I was sitting in the back of the classroom and I missed all the important things on the blackboard that I was supposed to write down. I could see things close to me but at any distance things got fuzzy. Kind of like life gets from time to time if you get to drifting along and let the important stuff get out of focus.

Did they move me to the front of the classroom?

No, they didn't, they put glasses on me.

Well, I guess I am slightly sidetracked from the point of this story, but I want to say that, I did the same with my first child, and with my second. That is, I didn't move them to the front, I put glasses on them. They both wear glasses today. This probably qualifies me as a very slow learner. By the third child I said, "No, no glasses, just put him in the front of the classroom."

This became a battle with the optometrist, my wife, and the school but I refused to back down.

He has 20/15 vision today.

Oh yeah, he is forty.

I don't think that is a coincidence

Anyway, for whatever reason, I wore glasses, and I hated them. Well, maybe hated is a tiny bit strong, but that was the era of Buddy Holley black or horn-rimmed glasses and I thought they looked dorky. The girls had those weird looking dark, kind of oriental shaped ugly frames too.

Where were Gucci and Prada in those days?

Then came the contact revolution. Now, mind you, contact lenses were invented in 1887 so it isn't that they weren't around, I just didn't know. Well, maybe nobody knew because it took almost one hundred years for someone to figure out how to make one that could be worn for more than an hour. I only became aware of them when I was fifteen. I wanted them.

There was an eye clinic in Tokyo that did hard contact lenses (this was long before soft lenses) and I talked my parents into letting me go to there to be fitted. It turned out that one of the officer's wives in our housing area wanted them also so this was great, an adult could accompany me, we made the trip together by train.

I must interrupt myself again here to say that you might think that with me being fifteen and the woman probably some ancient age like thirty that I really was accompanying her. You would be wrong. She had never taken the train to Tokyo and I had so, I figured out the train schedule, I bought us tickets, I got us a cab, and I got us to the clinic.

The first time we went there was for them to do that magic act that they have everywhere in the world that somehow ends with them knowing what lens to put in your eye. In addition, they had to take measurements of your eye to determine size and curvature, and well, I don't know what
else but I'm sure it was really important stuff. The optometrist didn't speak

English, so it took longer than normal as a translator had to explain everything we said to him and then everything he said back to us. Other than that, the first trip wasn't very memorable, it's the second that I
remember.

We had to wait three weeks after our measurement appointment before we could go for our final fitting, to get our contacts, to finally be free of the dreaded glasses.

Oh boy!

We arrived at the clinic in the morning. We were early, way early, for our appointments because we were quite sick of wearing glasses.

They weren't ready for us, so we had a seat in the main room. Now when I say main room, I truly mean it. You walked in the door and you were in this room. It's not like we are used to today with a waiting room that holds ten to forty people. This was warehouse size. It was at least ten thousand square feet.

No, I am not exaggerating, it was a

big open space with wall to wall floors, a few windows, chairs and treatment tables here and there. There must have been five hundred people in that room. They were everywhere. People from all walks of life, all Japanese. Strangely, I don't remember the room from my first visit, but it is vivid in my memory of the second time.

It wasn't just for waiting, and the clinic wasn't just for contacts, it was also for, well, all kinds of eye stuff, glasses, diseases of the eyes, cataracts, glaucoma, stuff like that. In addition to all the patients in the room, there were oodles of white coats poking, prodding, shining lights, waving
fingers in front of and doing all those ocular actions that are essential to finding out what your problems are or, well, certainly to making sure you feel like you are getting your money's worth and that the people who are treating you have some secret knowledge and are really competent.

What happened right next to us while we were waiting was something that I didn't understand then or now. A doctor, or at least a man in a white coat that I thought might be a doctor, was standing in front of a really old Japanese man who was sitting on a treatment table. The doctor had a large syringe in his hand. It had a needle about seven feet long on it. Well, in truth, it was probably only ten inches long but think about it, ten inches! He held it up right in front of the man's left eye just where it meets the nose, then started moving forward like he was going to poke it in there and then he, well, I don't know what he did because I looked away. I was horrified. What could that have been about? (actually, I do know now because I've had this procedure and the needle is long and it does get poked into your eye without any anesthesia or anything but an admonishment. 'don't move!' poke).

The fitting room for contacts was a private room. Or maybe we got a private room because we were American, the only Americans in the entire establishment. Now that I think about it, it was the head doctor's office. It was the only other room except for the main room. The doctor showed me my lenses. They were in this really cool gold case, shaped like a ball, that opened on both sides to reveal felt covered compartments. A green side and a red side.

The translator told me that the doctor was going to put them in my eyes for me to check the fit and because I hadn't been taught, yet, how to do it myself. So, I leaned back, and he leaned in.

He held my right eye open and put the lens in.

I fainted.

I woke up on the floor. The doctor was shouting, waving his arms in the air and acting quite agitated. The translator was not very happy. The doctor kept jabbering something at me. The translator informed me that the doctor was saying that I would not be getting contact lenses. He had taken the lens out while I was unconscious.

I got up, sat back down in the chair and said, "Put it back in."

The translator said that the doctor was adamant, I could not have lenses, I shouldn't be wearing lenses, I was not a candidate for lenses, I was too high strung, too young, too, well too something. He told

me that I had to leave. I just sat there shaking my head no. I told the translator to tell the doctor that I wasn't going anywhere until he put the lens back in. This
impasse continued until the doctor finally realized that I was going to take up the rest of his day if need be.

I was going to be wearing contacts.

I didn't faint when he put it in the second time which calmed him a bit. The left eye went well also. Then he put lenses into the eyes of the wife who was with me, who, not being the weakling that I was, had no problems.

We sat in the main room for a while. All kinds of strange things, like the man and the syringe, were still going on around us. We were looking for the hidden camera, well, of course, not really but, the whole scene was like that, except real. My eyes, well, our eyes were watering so badly we could barely see. I guess that is a normal reaction when you put this big of a piece of foreign matter in your eyes.

After about 30 minutes the translator came out and told us that we needed to keep the lenses in for about two to three hours more and why not go to lunch. Come back for a checkup in three hours.

Ok, lunch. We were almost blind, but we set off for lunch. Flagged down a cab. Cabs were plentiful, cheap, and fast in those days. We used to joke that they were all Kamikaze pilots who didn't get a chance to fly. It was a "taking your life in your hands" experience to take a cab in Tokyo in the fifties.

We managed to make enough hand gestures that the driver figured out we were hungry and dropped us at a Soba bar. Soba noodles are long thin noodles served in a soup, it was inexpensive and delicious, and the bars were plentiful. The restaurant was a sweet, tiny, hole-in-the-wall place with just six tables, simply but tastefully done like the Japanese are famous for.

I'm sure the menu contained other things but we couldn't read the it with the way our eyes were tearing, so we just ordered soba and green tea. Oh yes, Japanese green tea, delicate in color and in taste, supposedly very healthy for you, containing powerful antioxidants, reducing blood sugar, preventing cancer, well, the list goes on and on. I didn't know anything about that, I only knew that I really liked it. During my time in Japan is was my drink of choice whenever I ate in a Japanese restaurant and many times at home when brewed by our maids. I have never found it to be as good since leaving Japan.

After lunch it was the same ordeal. Stumble blindly into the street, flag down a cab, hold the back of the seat in terror because of the driving, go back to the clinic, and wait in the main room, crying, watching the show until our time was up.

As I recall I had to return to Tokyo a few times more to practice putting in and wearing the lenses. My eyes eventually stopped making so many tears (maybe that is why I have dry eye today).

I wore those lenses for at least ten years. I never really got used to them. They always used to float down to my lower lid causing me to blink, which moved them up again. Then they would float down again and, well, it was an endless cycle. What I found worked was to hold my head back at an angle so the lenses rested directly on my lower lid, so I didn't blink. It made me look kind of haughty, kind of like

I was looking down my nose at everyone.

It is a habit that forty years after I stopped using them, I still have.

I went from looking dorky to looking unapproachable, disdainful, and supercilious.

A huge improvement.

Hitchhiking

The high school I went to in Japan was located in a suburb of Tokyo. It was centrally located for those dependents who lived in the city and those who lived at the bases that were stretched around Tokyo in a crescent about an hour plus drive away. We rode the bus every day, an hour plus there and an hour plus back. It was necessary, but kind of boring. Well, we entertained ourselves and it did give us an hour to do the homework we should have done the night before.

Maybe it also accustomed us for later in life to participate in that great American tradition of commuting hours to work each day.

About a month before the end of my sophomore year, while riding the bus home one day, a friend started making obscene gestures. I thought he was being cute, so I copied him. No one stopped us so, we got bolder and bolder.

There are these moments in my life when I have done something and later, well, many times later, like the rest of my life later, when I remember them, I shake my head and wonder why, why, why. Things that fifty years later I am still ashamed of.

This was one of those.

We were kicked off the bus for the rest of the year.

This was a significant problem, a life changing problem. It was already more than an hour into Tokyo to the school on the school bus with no freeways. In reality at that time there weren't any real main roads and now I had to figure out how to get there and a way to do it.

If you are paying attention you have realized that at fifteen years old my parents had left me to fend for myself in a strange land. My only guidance was don't miss or be late for school.

Did I mention that I was treated like an adult? I think they thought of it as a learning experience.

It was but perhaps not as they intended.

While Japan had great public transportation, the ride by train into Tokyo, then by train out to the suburb where the school was located, then by bus to the base, and then walking into the school, was a three-hour ordeal.

Each way.

Wow, that last sentence kind of reminds me of "Destination Moon" by They Might Be Giants. "By rocket to the moon, by airplane to the rocket, by taxi to the airport, by..."

Sorry, back on track.

My parents, as they had all my life, let me make my own mistakes and live with them. My dad could have done something to help me. He had enough rank to make them let me back on the bus. He could have had someone drive me into school each day. Well, I guess that wouldn't really be termed help. That would be enabling me, sending me a message that I didn't really have to be responsible for my own actions because dad would save me. My parents never did that. They supported me but, as I said, I had to live with my own mistakes.

What I did for the next month was to take the base bus from home to the other side of the base, walk out the gate and start hitching.

You remember hitchhiking. Stand by the side of the road, put out your thumb, and try to flag a car down.

The problem was that the Japanese didn't understand a thumb stuck out. It would have been like trying to get a car to stop on an LA freeway. The other problem was there were very few cars, but tons of three wheelers, which were Japanese pickup trucks. Sort of. They were motorcycles with two back wheels over which there was a small truck bed. Noisy but efficient.

What I found worked was to jump out in front of the first passing three-wheeler, waving my arms, shouting, "chotto matte", which is Japanese for 'just a minute'. Then, when they stopped, I would go over to the driver and ask, "Doko iku no", which I had been taught meant 'where are you going'? He would respond in Japanese saying something that I, of course, couldn't understand but I would nod my head and reply, "daijobu" which is Japanese for 'okay' and then jump in the truck bed of his three-wheeler.

When he turned from the direction I wanted to go, I would rap on the cab of the truck shouting, "chotto matte" again until he stopped. Then I would climb out and look for the next ride.

Some of my rides were better than others, sometimes in a real car, sometimes on the way home from school I would meet a businessman who wanted to practice English. Once I got a ride with a man whose house was on my route who invited me in to share tea and sushi. One time I stopped a honey wagon. For those of you who don't know that term it was a wagon full of pots of the contents of toilets from the houses on the honey wagon man's route. Kind of like our trash men today but incredibly more pungent.

I never made that mistake again.

As I recall I was never late for school.

This whole experience turned out to be a blessing in disguise as I used this method, alone and with friends, to travel all over Japan during the rest of my time there. Of course, we used the trains and busses but, sometimes the best way to get there was to hitchhike.

Skullbusters

Smokey Johnson was my wrestling partner, but I don't remember his stage name. I wrestled under the name of "Wild Red Berry". My brother was "The Czech". This was 1958 and we had a professional wrestling team, twenty-two years before the World Wrestling Federation came into existence. This all came about because in the fall of 1957 I got into a discussion with a friend on the lawn of the teen club.

Every base in Japan had a teen club. This was a great place for teens to gather, with a reception area, bathrooms, an office for the Sargent who ran the club, a main room with a stage and a dance floor and tables surrounding it just like a night club, and activity rooms for well, whatever came up.

It was our own private club where all the teens on the base gathered almost every day after school and for sure on Friday and Saturday nights for dances. It was a hot spot for meeting up with the opposite sex, playing ping pong, pool, or hanging out. It had a sound system for dancing and a kitchen for catering food.

Oh yes one other thing, it was free.

The discussion we had on the lawn of the club was whether a boxer or a street fighter would prevail in a fight. I had been taking boxing lessons and my friend had grown up in some hard neighborhoods. He said a street fighter would beat a boxer every time. I disagreed. We weren't getting anywhere because we both believed that our opinion was the right one, not unlike most political discussions today.

The Sargent who ran the club stood watching us for quite a while before he finally suggested "why don't we just go over to the base gym and use the gloves and the ring to put this to the test?"

It was to have been a five-round fight, in a regulation ring, using 10-ounce gloves. Half of the teens on base had followed us to the gym to see us fight. After three rounds I could barely hold my hands up and I thought I was going to die I was so exhausted. I was trying to use what I had been taught like keeping my guard up, jabbing, using one-two combinations, and keep looking for an opening. My friend just came in swinging, right, left, right, left, and didn't stop. He was beating the crap out of me and I was too stupid, or too macho to quit.

I had just gotten braces on my teeth and we weren't wearing mouth protection, so by the end of the third round I was bleeding profusely from my mouth all over my gloves, all over my opponent, all over my shirt and all over the mat.

Mercifully, the Sergeant stopped the fight. Thank god because I was losing badly. Even the most biased or incompetent judge wouldn't have given me that decision.

That should have been the end of my fighting career, but the Sergeant had a plan. He asked us if we wanted to really learn some moves, how to fight but not really fight, how to take a hit or a fall and not get hurt. He was talking about wrestling.

Now in our minds, at the time, wrestling was kind of a strange boring looking sport where two guys kind of grappled with each other for a while until the Ref said one of them was the winner. It seemed about as interesting as Sumo wrestling.

Sarge patiently explained that what he was talking about was a show. An exciting show where there were lots of punches, kicks, and throws. Throws and moves with really cool names like the airplane spin, brainbuster, head scissors takedown, and the back-body drop. He said that in New Orleans, where he came from, a small group of guys were putting together shows, wearing outrageous costumes, doing all kinds of these crazy maneuvers, and people were paying to come see them and believing, well, at least pretending to believe that, it was real.

Now he had our attention. We were teenage boys, awash with testosterone. Something that we could do that involved fighting but not really getting hurt, where you might have adoring fans, and get paid, this was the ultimate fantasy, well one of them anyway. Show us where to sign up!

"Not so fast, fellows," he said, "first you have to learn the basics." How to fake a punch and make it look real, how to get thrown over someone's shoulder or even from over their head and land and not get hurt, how to lift someone heavier than you into a throw, in short, how-to put-on a really good show that looks like real fighting but wasn't. How to look like you had almost died when you hadn't.

We started in one of the activity rooms at the teen club on mats learning jujitsu. Then we progressed to showmanship. We learned how to slam our bodies on the mat but break the fall, how to throw, how to lift, how to punch, how to take a fall, and how to "pin" an opponent.

Oh yeah "pin".

There is nothing magical about this "pinning" thing, it's still done the same way today. Somehow after a half hour of throwing each other around and dishing out and receiving incredible amounts of punishment, punishment that would have put any normal human out of commission permanently, and then having some tantalizing close calls where one wrestler or the other almost "pins" the other, the match ends because one guys shoulders are on the mat for a count of three.

How lame is that? I mean really it's one of the things that makes it impossible for me to watch professional wrestling today. How normally rational human beings can disengage their minds in order to believe that something like this is real is way out of my circle of understanding.

It's sort of like the movies where one guy has a twenty-ton truck fall on him but somehow manages to crawl out from under, unscathed, and capture the bad guy. I guess we suspend our belief for the entertainment of it all. Anyway the "pin" was preordained. Who would win and when and how was decided before the match began. It was a show after all.

Our next step was developing our wrestling persona. There had to be good guys and bad guys, clean cut types and real scumbags, guys who fought fairly and guys who fought dirty, well, dirty when the audience could see but not, of course, when the ref could.

I chose my name based on a real wrestler at the time, "Wild Red Berry". I didn't know that he was real at the time, the Sarge told me about him and I believed him. It turns out that if you search the internet for him, he really existed, lived in New Orleans and did in fact put on wrestling shows. I kind of embellished his character a bit. First off, I wanted to be a bad guy but, the kind of guy that the crowd loves to hate. A guy too full of his own importance, needing an entourage around him to prop up his own ego and self-worth. People to carry, run errands, fetch, idolize, fawn over, and be yes men to the great one.

Sounds like an awful lot of politicians and pop stars today.

Our seamstress (yes, we had a seamstress) made me a cape and a beret. I stood in the back yard of our house with a washtub over a wood fire and dyed clothes red. Red jeans, red shorts, red sweatshirts. I got some friends to participate. I had a manager, an assistant manager, an assistant assistant manager, and a guy whose duty was to come out before the match and spray red perfume around from a red atomizer. The guys all wore the red clothes with my name and their position embroidered on them. The pre-show with my entourage sometimes took longer than the match.

I always wrestled Smokey and after almost pinning him a bunch of times it was pre-ordained that I would lose easily, except for one time when I chopped him in the Adams apple and nearly killed him and had to fool around until he recovered enough to become the winner. Smokey was a great big guy and I was kind of wimpy. He would lift me easily over his head, swirl me around in an airplane spin, slam me on the mat and voila, PIN.

Looking back with the wisdom of fifty years and having seen a few current day professional bouts, the whole thing was pretty silly, but at the time it was a lot of fun. We put on shows for free to start with and then as we got better, managed to get booked into the Johnson and Yakota Officer's clubs several times where we were paid for performing.

I'm not sure why but we became the warm-up act for the main show on Wednesday stag night which, of course, was the strip show. I remember noticing at the time that we didn't seem to hold the attention of the heavy drinking crowd that just wanted our show to end so that the good stuff could start.

We named the team "JAB (Johnson Air Base) Skullbusters" and used the money we were paid to buy team jackets.

That jacket is one of the few things I still have from my time in Japan. It is a black wool jacket with white leather inserts at the shoulders and white wool stretch cuffs and collar. A few years ago, my brother "The Czech" had the cuffs and collar redone because of moth damage so the jacket is in mint condition with a big human skull embroidered on the back, emblazoned with "Skullbusters"

I can still wear it.

Drinking Game

I can't tell you the number of times I came home from school and found my parents playing 'the drinking game'. Well, I'm calling it 'the drinking game' because I don't know the real name of this game. It is a Japanese game and I'm sure it doesn't translate to 'the drinking game'.

Most probably the translation is 'the singing game' because if you "lose" (and I put lose in big quotations because in this game losing is really winning), you are forced to sing a song. Otherwise you must drink a cup of sake (a wine made from rice). There are six sides to the die that you throw when playing. Five of them labeled A to E with the sixth being a musical staff. There are five cups, A being the smallest and E being the largest that you must drink from whenever that letter comes up.

The winner (or loser depending on your point of view) is the musical staff. Roll that and you need only sing.

Anyway, I would come home to this activity in full swing. Mom and Dad and two or three maids around the dining room table, a small bottle of sake on the table, a five-liter bottle on the stove and everyone in a jovial mood. Well, jovial is a euphemism for drunk. Most of the times I played, I joined after I got home from school, which with the hour bus ride and then a stop at the teen club was four thirty, five. They had been playing since just after lunch and were all completely smashed.

Of course, I joined in and got smashed also.

Usually this game continued until we were out of sake at which point, I went off to bed and passed out. The strange thing is that most nights my parents went off to the Officer's Club where they continued to party. It wasn't until later in life that I understood how one could consume that much alcohol and still function.

Omi River

The spring snow melt created raging class 3 and class 4 rapids on the Omi river. We had been told by others who had been there that it was a rafter's dream. Big rocks, dangerous currents, fairly steep mini-falls, whirlpools, eddies, steep gradients, holes, narrow bridge passages, and some straight calmer stretches to give you a chance to catch your breath. Incredibly beautiful and completely wild scenery that could be enjoyed without anyone else around or in your way. Great places to stop and picnic and swim.

Not to be missed.

Ok those of you who are experts about class 3 or 4 rapids or even those who have been on them are probably shaking your heads and saying what in the hell are 15 and 16-year-old kids doing on a course like that. Maybe you are assuming we had guides.

No, we didn't.

Experience?

No.

Anything other than 15-year-old mentality?

Sadly no.

We heard about this gem of a river because we had a raft. Because our maid was dating a sergeant in supply who brought my brother and I a six-man raft that was to have been used by pilots who had to ditch at sea. Sort of a surplus item, well perhaps an "it fell off the truck" gift to get in my dad's good graces. My dad had a lot of influence about who our maids could date.

Friends who had gone before said that the river would be a perfect place to use the raft.

Four of us went by train, bus and finally we hitchhiked (see hitchhiking) to get there. It was a beautiful spring day, temperatures in the high 60's, sunny, water temperature about 60.

I noticed on the final road along the river that every house on the bank of the river had an outhouse and every outhouse had a tube that emptied into the river. We were kids; it didn't seem to matter at the time, the water looked clear, I mean how bad could it be?

If anything, the descriptions of how wild the river was were understated, it looked like almost solid whitewater. It looked really exciting and like it was going to be a lot of fun.

We didn't bring a lot of stuff. We only had the raft and a lunch of sorts, not much clothing. We were wearing shorts, tee shirts and zori. The raft had a handle that once you pulled it, inflation took only about 15 seconds. Within minutes of deciding where to put in we were ready to go. Pull the handle, wow, instant raft.

Had we walked the river? No.

Had we made contingency plans? No.

Had we discussed jobs, hierarchy, bailouts, what we meant by stop, start, right, left, over here, over there, well, anything beyond "let's go"?

NO.

The four of us climbed in and shoved off. The very first challenge was a huge bolder with a mini-fall that we took dead on. The water was going over it and we did too, throwing my brother about ten feet in the air and into the water. The rest of us paddled for shore and then jumped out to beach the raft to allow my brother to catch up. The next two raging rapids with right and left turns ended up throwing all of us into the water but holding on for dear life. We were having fun and it never crossed our minds that we were in danger.

After about five minutes of "oh my god I think we are going to die" water, things smoothed out. We had less than a minute to catch our breath. Ahead of us was a very narrow section spanned by a bridge. The bridge had the shore, a very narrow space, then a pylon, a wider space, another pylon, a very narrow space, and then the other shore. The space between the two main pylons was about, well just a bit wider than the raft if we maneuvered it straight in.

I asked my brother "What do you think, should we go for it?" He looked at me then at the bridge, then at me and said, "I don't know, what do you think?"

We had as much time as you just had to read the above sentence to make a decision. The decision had been made for us. We were going for it.

Now all those rehearsals, all that practice, all our planning well, total lack of rehearsals, practice, and planning was about to pay off. I screamed left, right, back, stop, wait, go back, over here, over there, oh shit we're going to die.

My last words were, "Don't jump to the high side when we hit the pylon."

Everyone, including myself, jumped to the upstream side of the raft (the high side) as we hit the bridge. That forced it under the water wrapping the raft right around the pylon.

We all ended up on the bridge. The raft was wrapped on the pylon and our combined strength wouldn't even budge it. Our lunch was gone. Our day was over after less than fifteen minutes of rafting. We were all fine which couldn't be said for the raft.

We left it and trudged up the narrow dirt road, wet, tired, and dispirited to the main road to make our way home.

* * *

Three weeks later we had a plan. We convinced the teen club to have an excursion by bus for a picnic day. We convinced the driver that the perfect place would be this lovely spot by the Omi. We planned to get the raft back.

This time there were about sixteen of us, drinks, food, changes of clothing, and, oh yes, girls.

When we got there, it turned out we really didn't have a plan. We had no idea, other than brute strength, how to pull the raft out and brute strength even with eight of us wasn't working. We found an old piece of stranded cable and managed to tie it around the raft. The girls sat on the bank eating the picnic lunch while eight guys stood on the opposite bank playing tug-of-war with a raft.

The raft won. We were beaten.

Then, just when we had finally given up, along came this old Japanese farmer on an even older tractor. He was making his way across the narrow bridge when we flagged him down and asked his help, well maybe asked is a stretch, but we managed to gesture at the raft and the cable and our pulling and his tractor and he got the idea.

We hooked the cable to the tractor and the raft came right off.

After saying "Domo arigato gozaimasu" (Japanese for: thank you very much) dozens of times and sending the farmer on his way, we looked at the raft. Three weeks had aged it about a hundred years. It was deflated, ripped in places, with a hole in the bottom, and a fist sized hole in the inflatable side. It was going to need some major repairs.

We spent the rest of the day picnicking, flirting around with the girls, and swimming in a quiet deep hole just below the bridge that turned out to be perfect, if you forgot about the outhouses, that is. I ended up with a girl my age that I dated off and on for the rest of my time in Japan and even saw once after returning to the states. A perfect day, I fell asleep in her lap on the bus ride home.

The next day I unrolled the raft out in the back yard of our home. I didn't have a clue where to start. The sergeant who had given it to me took one look at it and said that he thought he knew where he could get it repaired.

He took it away and came back the next day with a brand new one. Evidently you just turn in an old one to get a new one, much easier than finding one that has fallen off the truck.

I kept that raft in its uninflated pristine condition until we returned to the States where it too enjoyed quite some adventures.

The sergeant ended up marrying our maid Nobuko.

Racism

Wait.

Before you start reading this section, I have to warn you that, of course, I'm prejudiced. If you can't handle that, skip this section.

I am personally prejudiced against those people who have no tolerance for other people who are different than they are. I try hard not to be but, it's hard to ignore ignorance and stupidity. Wow, ignorance and stupidity, that sounds kind of intolerant, doesn't it? That's exactly what I just said, I'm prejudiced.

In our country there are these huge divisions, between everything and everyone, that don't make rational sense.

I guess that's it.

Prejudice doesn't make sense. It's not supposed to because it's not based on logic. It's based on things that you were taught as a child, on biases and preconceived notions that you got from someone else, usually your parents.

Everyone hates everyone else who isn't exactly the same as
They are.

I am reminded of a joke that I heard a few years ago, well quite a few years ago, by Emo Phillips, which is funny and extremely sad at the same time. I have included this sad funny joke as a footnote. (see footnote 1)

Wait, again. Stop and skip to the bottom and read the joke. I want you to get the point I am trying to make so you need to read it now.

Thanks.

The point of this joke is that not only can we not get along with those who are radically different than we are; we don't even have tolerance for people who are nearly exactly as we are.

What's that all about?

Growing up as a military brat meant that you were constantly thrown into situations where you met, worked with, lived with, went to school with, or were best friends with all kinds of different

people. Different races, different educational levels, different social skills, different intelligence,
different religions, different freckles, different toenails, different dress, well, I guess I could go on for another hundred differences or so, but you get the idea.

As a kid I wasn't aware that differences made a difference. For that I must credit my parents.

Which brings me to the point of this memory.

We lived in a single-family unit in the base housing annex of Johnson Air Force Base near Tokyo, Japan from 1955 to 1958. Our unit was located at the top of a hill at the back of the complex, beautiful, isolated and quite large. We had five bedrooms, living room, dining room, kitchen, mud room, and three bathrooms.

I think my dad was single-handedly trying to help bring back the after-war economy so, we had two live in maids, another maid that came every day, a houseboy, a seamstress, and a gardener.

It seemed normal at the time.

My parents had the master bedroom, the two maids had another, my sister had one, our two younger brothers had one, and my brother, who was 13 months younger, and I shared the last bedroom.

The base was a small community which meant that all of us teenagers were a close-knit group. We rode the bus together, we went to the teen club together, we played together, we partied together. Black, white, brown, green, short, fat, stupid, boring, lazy, we were all friends, we lived together.

One night I had a slumber party at our house. There were about twelve of us. Just guys. We drank coke, played cards, fooled around, watched Sumo wrestling on TV (which was about the only program you could get then), and just had a normal teenage good time.

Then we went to bed. We all had to share the one bedroom.

Eight guys slept on the floor. My brother and a friend of his slept in his twin bed and my friend Jasper and I slept in mine. Totally uncomfortable but we were kids, we didn't know any better.

You remember.

Those good old days when you could put your head down on a pillow and fall instantly asleep anywhere no matter what and wake up eight or ten hours later.

In the morning after everyone had left, I came into my room and found one of the maids changing the sheets on my bed.

This didn't make sense.

I mean I know we had all these maids without enough to do but, they had just changed the sheets the day before.

I have never been one to let sleeping dogs lie, leave well enough alone, live and let live, well, there are certainly more of those but, the point is I have always wanted to know the why behind everything so, I asked the maid, "Why are you changing my sheets?"

"Because Ojii-san told me they dirty", she replied.

Ojii-san is the Japanese word for grandfather and my dad had adopted it as his name. "They dirty" made no sense to me, aside from the fact that she was Japanese and didn't speak perfect English, so I confronted my dad and asked him what was going on.

His response was, "Well, Jasper slept in that bed last night."

"Yes dad, but so did I," I pointed out.

"I know but they're dirty," he said, with this really guilty look on his face.

"The sheets?" I questioned.

"No, you know, them," he answered.

"Them?" I repeated, "Them who?"

"You know, them," he reiterated. Then he used the N word.

Oh my god. I was poleaxed. He meant Jasper, my friend. My friend who was black. "Them" meant black people in general.

I was sixteen years old and I never knew. They had kept this from me for all these years. They had not indoctrinated me with what must have been really deep-seated biases. They had these notions and somehow they had not even once hinted to their children that someone different, someone not like us, someone with a different skin color might not be as good as them. Inferior. No, not just inferior, rather more like someone or something really horrible.

I was disappointed in my dad. It was one of those life changing moments when I lost some of that blind, unwavering, "these are my parents and everything they do or say is the absolute truth", belief.

I was sick with the knowledge. I hated what had happened to how I felt about them. I hated that this big chasm had opened between us. I was angry.

What was this all about?

That's not what you taught me.

Damit anyway, why are you saying this now?

Did I say I was angry, confused, hurt, lost, disappointed, sick at heart?

Yes.

I have to say, years later, the fact that my parents managed to keep from imprinting their prejudice on me, is one of the proudest memories I have of them.

1

I was walking across a bridge one day, and I saw a man standing on the edge, about to jump off. So, I ran over and said, "Stop! Don't do it!"

"Why shouldn't I?" he said.

I said, "Well, there's so much to live for!"

He said, "Like what?"

I said, "Well, are you religious or an atheist?"

He said, "Religious."

I said, "Me too! Are you Christian or Buddhist?"

He said, "Christian."

I said, "Me too! Are you Catholic or Protestant?"

He said, "Protestant."

I said, "Me too! Are you Episcopalian or Baptist?"

He said, "Baptist!"

I said, "Wow! Me too! Are you Baptist Church of God or Baptist Church of the Lord?"

He said, "Baptist Church of God!"

I said, "Me too! Are you Original Baptist Church of God or are you Reformed Baptist Church of God?"

He said, "Reformed Baptist Church of God!"

I said, "Me too! Are you Reformed Baptist Church of God, Reformation of 1879, or Reformed Baptist Church of God, Reformation of 1915?"

He said, "Reformed Baptist Church of God, Reformation of 1915!"

I said, "Die, heretic scum!" and pushed him off.

Emo Phillips (1985)

Port Wine

The demon rum was ridiculously easy to get in Japan.

Well not just rum. Beer, wine, sake, gin, vodka, scotch, whiskey, and that horrible Japanese version of whiskey called Suntory which you can still buy today. Oh my god for my unsophisticated palette it was really bad, but ridiculously easy to get.

Actually, since we were kids, we drank Suntory because it was the cheapest. Let me put that in perspective. I could go to the base annex exchange (precursor to Seven Eleven) and buy a fifth of Gordon's gin for ninety cents. Yes, I could actually buy it on the base.

Suntory was cheaper.

As for buying booze at 14 or 15, this was never a problem. We didn't need an adult to buy it for us. To the Japanese we looked like we were in our twenties. We just walked into any store that sold intoxicants and slapped down our money.

One night, when I was fifteen, six of us decided to have a guy's party. The housing area where we lived was located in a hilly area with high places, where there were houses, and low places, where there were ravines and plenty of places for us to hide and to get into trouble.

We were going to camp out, but we needed some liquids to spice up the night.

This was easy. We slipped out the back gate, down the hill, past the first red light in town that marked the first of many cathouses and stopped at the local liquor store. Well, it was really just a dingy small dirty hovel of a bar, that sold bottles. That night we decided to go upscale so we bought six bottles of Port wine.

At least we were told it was Port wine. It came in unmarked bottles and the corks were sticking out so you could easily uncork them.

We paid less than a dollar for six bottles of wine. We were ready to party.

Back in the ravine we set up six pup tents, lit a small fire, and started drinking and trading lies. Almost right away two of the guys decided they didn't like the taste. Great! That just meant more for the rest of us. About halfway into my bottle I really started to feel good, kind of funny, lightheaded, but good. This feeling was great, and I just knew that if I drank some more I'd feel even better. So, I did. I have had that feeling more than once since then, it always seems right at the time but, it never has been.

We were getting kind of loud and the two guys not drinking thought we were acting stupid. What did they know? We were having fun, singing songs, baying at the moon, screaming to see who could scream the loudest. Normal stuff. They asked us to keep it down. Then some of the
people in the houses at the top of the ravine started hollering at us to keep it down also.

Hey, maybe we were being too loud.

The four of us still drinking finished our bottles and started passing the remaining two bottles back and forth. I was having trouble walking, actually I was having trouble even standing, and somehow keeping quiet was impossible. The two sober friends left, completely disgusted with us. The neighbors were complaining steadily.

Then a sobering thing happened. My father showed up. He didn't yell at me, he wasn't mad angry or incensed, he just told me, quietly, that I had to come home with him.

So, there I was, quiet now, chastised, realizing I was in trouble, walking behind my dad. Well, walking is maybe too elegant of a description. There I was zigzaging, falling down, having trouble focusing on where we were, behind my dad, trying to get back to our house.

Maybe we were having those earthquakes that Japan is famous for. Something was causing the ground to move around, making it hard to walk. Dad didn't seem to be having any trouble. I wasn't feeling too well. What happened to that really good feeling?

When I got home my dad asked me to come into his bedroom so he could talk to me. Not much talking got done, at least by them, as I promptly went into their bathroom and emptied the contents of my stomach into their toilet. I spent most of the night there. Somehow, I felt the need to confess so, in between bouts of heaving, I told them all my secrets. I can't imagine what I was thinking of, it must have been the demon rum, well, port wine.

I vowed that I would never never do that again, which of course was hubris.

To this day, however, I still cannot drink port wine.

House of Ill Repute

One of the rights of passage, when I was a teenager, was for some of the braver, or stupider, guys to sneak out on a spring night and make a journey to a local whorehouse to have your first "real" sexual experience.

It was an opportunity to find out what all the mystery was about. It was a chance to look at and maybe touch those secret, forbidden places that occupied so much of our teen-age waking and sleeping thoughts.

Those who had gone before us bragged about how incredible, how exciting, how mysterious it was. It would be the experience of a lifetime.

Or so we were told.

Johnson Air Force Base, where my dad was stationed, was located next to the small town of Irumagawa, Japan, and because there were thousands of lonely airmen stationed there, there were, of course, whorehouses.

They weren't hidden.

Everyone, including us teenagers, knew exactly where they were. Actually, they were quite well marked with traditional red lights. Red lights that were welcome signs for the thousands who, with no partner to be intimate with, and possessing very little chance or opportunity of finding one, used them as a substitute. Those houses did a thriving business day and night.

One spring night, during my junior year of high school, while dad and mom were at the Officers Club (which dad ran and my mom was forever playing hostess at), I met up with two friends to head out to a local bordello to become a man, to have sex with a woman, to get laid, to join the ranks of guys who had really done it, who had gone all the way with a girl.

We lived in the officers housing annex of the base called Hyde Park. It was pretty nice for base housing with some multi-family units and a few single-family units for the higher-ranking officers. There were lots of open spaces, lots of lawn, and some great ravines where we could get out of sight and into trouble.

Just out the back gate of this annex and a short walk down the hill brought you to the small town of Irumagawa, a typical small Japanese town of about 4000 inhabitants. Essentially there was just the one main street, teeming with kids, three wheelers (the Japanese substitute for a pickup
truck at the time), bicycles, hundreds of people on foot, carts, dogs, a few cars, and honey wagons.

* * *

Oh yes, honey wagons. After the war in Japan there was a booming business in human excrement. There were no central waste disposal systems, so every town had a honey wagon man. His job was to go around each evening and collect the remains from everyone's outhouses or "benjos". The waste, termed night-soil, which I never understood because some of us soiled during the day, was collected in gallon size wooden buckets with lids that leaked, badly.

There were often several hundred of these buckets loaded on a groaning cart pulled by a small horse or donkey. The smell was horrible. You knew for at least a mile away that you were approaching a honey wagon.

After collecting the waste from homes, the honey wagon man would then sell the contents to the local farmers to use as fertilizer on their fields. It was a prosperous business. Shunned by the community at large, the honey wagon man was always one of the richest men in any town.

The town also had all manner of shops, small grocery stores, shoe shops, pachinko parlors, street vendors selling yakitori and rice balls, pots and pans, clothing, udon and soba noodle soup bars, rice paper shops, bars, and the all-important whorehouses.

Going into town the first house with a red light was actually one of the first buildings on the path down to Irumagawa, conveniently located for those airmen who didn't have the will power, or the energy, or the money to walk farther into town to something maybe a bit more upscale.

So, here we were, on a school night, sneaking out of our homes to join up for our trip to the local brothel. Well, sneaking isn't exactly right. It was Japan and we were teenagers which, at that time, meant we were treated like adults. Our parents were busy, and the culture was safe. No one paid attention. We were kings and queens and we knew it.

So, really, here we were getting together, joking, laughing, and just walking out the back gate, down the hill and knock, knock, can we come in? The only thing you really needed to enter a cathouse in Japan was money.

This became the big problem.

Among the three of us we only had 400 yen and I had none. A "short time" (this implies that there were longer times but frankly we didn't have a clue what the other times were and really at that age how long were we going to last anyway) at that time was 200 yen which was only a little more than 50 cents. The mama-san who ran the place was adamant. No credit.
That meant that only two of us could have sex. The girls didn't exactly resemble the girls of my dreams, but boy did I want to do this. I begged and pleaded with my friends to lend me their money, to let me be one of the ones this week and the next

time I promised I would repay them and help them, just please, please, please, let it be me.

Hormones ruled and I lost.

We finally negotiated with the mama-san that, at least, I would be allowed to go into the room with my one friend and "watch". It wasn't ideal but my turn to have this first in a lifetime experience was to be the next time, in about two weeks, when we could make this trip again.

I was really fired up. I wasn't going to actually do it but, at least, I would get to see everything. A naked woman, breasts, secret places, and, the actual act. If I couldn't do it at least I could participate vicariously. I was ready!

Reading this paragraph is going to take you longer than what actually happened. The "girl" (well, a woman of about 30 which by the standards of 15 year old boys was ancient) turned off the lights. It was dark, very dark. I couldn't even see my hand (which is not what I was looking for), there was some fumbling, oh oh oh oh oh, groan, fumbling, and the lights came back on.

That's it? My buddy seemed happy, but I really felt cheated. What happened to sitting next to each other for a while and looking, touching, kissing? Lots of kissing. Where was the exploration of breasts, taking off the bra, the naked female body, and finally arriving at that, well, that other place? Where was the romance, the foreplay, the titillation, the arousal, the stuff that even at 15 I knew ought to be there?

Did I say I felt cheated?

Yes, I did. On another hand, I still wanted to have been the one, to have done it, to have become a man, or at least what I thought men were supposed to want and be.

Well lucky me.

Before the next time we could get away both of my friends were diagnosed with syphilis.

Rampant in local whorehouses we were told. How could we be have been so stupid?

Luckily a friendly corpsman at the base hospital treated them on the sly and their parents never found out.

I didn't go back.

Maybe it was this experience, maybe the things my parents taught me about girls and sex and how it should be, or maybe it was just bad timing. Whatever happened I knew that I didn't want fumble, oh oh oh oh, groan, fumble. I wanted it to be something more, something beautiful, something that meant something to both people.

Oh, I still wanted it. Badly. Thoughts about sex and how to get someone in bed still occupied most of my sleeping and waking time. I was a teenager, after all. I never acted on them until one night when I was twenty-one when I had my first "real" experience.

Different story.

Communal Hot Baths

During my time in Japan the Japanese were famous for their communal hot baths. Well, they still are it's just that things have changed a little.

Every major hotel, every small town had one. It was a place not only to get clean but to relax and sometimes visit with strangers.

By communal I mean men and women together without wearing any type of bathing attire.

Sadly, when I went back to Japan in the late 90's to visit my son who was stationed there in the marine corps, they no longer existed. I know that in very small remote towns they were still to be found and at the traditional hot spring's locations, but in the main things have been westernized.

That is to say that our western prudishness has injected itself into their culture such that all the hot baths at hotels were segregated. In fact, if you asked a young person about co-ed communal baths, they would swear that they never existed.

They did and I enjoyed them everywhere we went. Whenever dad took the family somewhere for an outing one of the first things my brother and I did was to search out the onsen (which is Japanese for 'hot springs' but has come to include the man-made bath houses also).

Basically, it is a hot, sometimes very uncomfortably hot large pool of mineral water. The mineral content can vary at different baths so much that the water can go from almost clear to so dark that you can't see your fingers when your hand is only submerged up to your wrist.

We were in a hotel on the Chiba peninsula (located on the other side of Tokyo Bay from Tokyo) one weekend that had beautiful onsen in a patio area. As soon as we checked in, my brother Baird and I threw on yukata's and headed for the bath.

The proper ritual for entering an onsen is to strip off your yukata, use one of the wooden buckets provided to wet yourself, soap your body clean, another bucket of water to rinse off and then enter the tub. When we arrived, there was only one other person in the water, a very old mama-san who was submerged up to her neck.

I mean she was in it, so it probably wasn't too hot.

We went through the ritual and then tried to get into the tub. The water was so hot that it took fifteen minutes of getting in a little and then out and throwing more water on us and then repeating before we were finally able to be submerged up to our waists.

About that time an older Japanese guy came onto the patio, dropped his yukata, splashed one bucket half-heartedly on himself, stepped in and submerged himself up to his neck.

I think he was showing off.

What was strange about all my forays into onsen during my time in Japan is that I was never titillated but once. Now, most probably this was because there were never girls my age in any. Certainly, the thirty and forty and fifty-year-old women that I encountered did nothing for me.

The one time was when dad took the whole family including two of the maids to Nagoya (on the other side of Mt Fuji almost to Kyoto, a five- or six-hour drive from Johnson Air Base) and we all went into a private onsen at the posh hotel we were staying at. I was surprised that our maid, Nobuko, who was easily at least thirty years old (and thus ancient by my standards) caught my attention. I noticed that I wasn't alone as my dad quickly submerged before he could embarrass himself.

Tokens

Gambling is not a new phenomenon.
I'm sure it is just as old as the world's
oldest profession which, of course, is food
preparation. Well, I guess there are
different theories about the world's oldest
profession. Maybe profession is the wrong
word and I'm really thinking of activities.
Anyway eating, drinking, having sex, and
gambling must be like the chicken and the
egg. No one really knows which one came
first but gambling is right up there.

Throwing your money away for no
good reason seems to be one of those god
given rights that people with a bit of cash
in their pocket, and many times those with
none, feel is a necessary activity to prove
that they are alive, whole, in control, larger
than life, real, or they need the rush,
or maybe just the feeling that they won't be
able to pay their rent in the morning. For
whatever reason people gamble,
sometimes without meaning to or even
knowing why.

There was gambling everywhere in
Japan, well, to be fair there was and is
gambling everywhere in the world. People
don't seem to be able to function without

it. It is a pervasive theme throughout every culture.

For the Japanese it is pachinko. The Japanese love pachinko. Pachinko parlors were everywhere. I could go into Irumagawa, a town of 4000 people, on the main street, and play pachinko. Walk in off the busy street into a small room with perhaps 50 machines. Buy some pachinko balls, sit down and play. They were crude machines with nails for pegs and basic flippers to throw the balls, but it was a place to sit and gamble. The parlors were always busy.

Of course, the American version of that type of machine was the slot machine, also known as the one-armed bandit. A fairly simple upright machine that you put coins into then pulled a lever on the right side that spun three reels. If the reels lined up in a configuration that payed off you got some coins back, if they didn't the machine kept your money. It should come as no surprise that the machine kept more money than it gave back.

After all it was a bandit.

My dad had slots at the Officer's Club that he ran. Very tasteful room, very understated, very elegant, well, elegant for a casino, but clearly there for one purpose. To relieve you of your loose change, to free you of those bulging wads of bills in your pocket, to make your trip home a little more interesting as you wondered how it was you were going to explain to your loving wife what had happened to your check.

Check, well, dad didn't really get a check. He got what was referred to as funny money, sort of like Monopoly money but better made.

After the war the military issued Military Payment Certificates, known as MPC, for use as money. It took the place of US dollars in our overseas bases. My dad received his pay in MPC and could then convert it into Yen to purchase goods and services in the local economy but, the trick was it was only a one-way conversion. You could not convert Yen back into MPC. This was supposed to insulate the US dollar and make it difficult or harder for black marketers to function. Well, that was the theory and I'm sure it must have slowed them up a tiny bit.

Naturally what happened was that when it was determined that so much MPC had gotten into the local economy that everyone was using it like real money, the solution was to replace it. This effectively meant that about every three years our government would declare that the current issue of MPC was not good anymore and would replace it with another series. Only those who legally could have MPC could change it to the new series, and then only up to the amount that you possibly could have been expected to have.

This created some very creative scrambling and a reverse black market as those black marketeers who had the, soon to be old series, frantically scurried to sell it at a discount back to anyone who had the right to convert it into the new series.

The same was true with the tokens (not real quarters) that were used in the casinos. To thwart the black marketeers these too were changed about every three years. With MPC, which were made of paper, it was very easy just to burn the old ones. With tokens, which were some kind of locally minted coin, that had the name "Johnsons Officers Club" on them a much more inventive scheme was used.

Well, I think it was an invention of my dad.

In the spring of 1958, the Johnson Officers Club changed their tokens. This meant that my dad had hundreds of thousands of quarter sized coins that had to be disposed of. A whole trunk full of coins. We had an old 55 Buick, so the trunk was quite large but, it was overflowing with tokens.

Now you might think that the right way to dispose of them would be to find someone who had a really hot furnace to melt them down. Someone who made glass or ornamental iron or maybe a place that made Samurai swords, well, after the war there wasn't much call for Samurai swords but, at least a place where the coins would be changed from their useful form.

My dad's solution was to load all of us in the car for a day trip with the coins in the trunk. We drove somewhere north of Johnson and toward the coast. We stopped at a bridge that was spanning a river that emptied into the Pacific. Then we just carried bagsful and handsful of coins and threw them into the river. It wasn't very deep so some of them could still be seen, some of them didn't quite make the river and ended up on the bank.

Dad said not to worry it was good enough.

Have you ever gotten tired of doing something that started out as fun? Let me tell you throwing away a few hundred thousand dollars, even if they were just tokens, is hard work. I got bored long before we were done. I took a break toward the end and let my dad finish.

This has only happened a few times in my life where having fun, really having fun turned out to be hard work and I took a break. It is a mistake that I try not to repeat because, when you look back, you realize that they were once in a lifetime deals, something that you should have continued to savor as that particular chance, that particular circumstance will never be yours again.

One last thing, I did a search on the internet while I was writing this and found someone selling a genuine "Johnsons Officers Club" token for $5.95.

We must have thrown away more than ten million dollars' worth at that rate.

Who knew?

Sixteenth Birthday

In October of 1957 my parents asked me what I wanted for my sixteenth birthday. I think they were thinking maybe I wanted something like clothes, or a bike, or something really simple like a dinner at the Officers club. I told my dad that what I wanted was for him to take me to Tokyo.

I wanted to stay in a Japanese style hotel for the weekend. I wanted to go to the Tokyo Onsen (the largest and most popular of the many hot baths in Tokyo at the time), to the Nichigeki Theater, and to a strip club.

My parents, who were not normal parents, at least when it came to things they thought proper for a teenage son, thought it was a great idea and so my sixteenth birthday trip was born.

Dad decided that this would be a trip for just guys so he and I and my 15-year-old brother packed our bags for my big adventure in Tokyo.

It was easy. We just jumped on a train at the station that was just a short walk outside of the gate of the housing annex where we lived. One-half hour and we were in Tokyo. The Japanese trains were then (and now) fast, clean, and on time.

From the train station it was a short taxi ride to our hotel, located in the "Ginza". World famous now as the most exclusive and expensive shopping and eating area in Japan, with the most expensive real estate on earth, even then it was a great shopping and entertainment district.

In Japan today, Japanese style hotels or even Japanese style rooms are almost impossible to find, but, in the 50's, they were plentiful. We checked into an upscale hotel which meant that, in addition to the big main room with tatami mats and a central table with hibachi, it also had en-suite American style toilets.

Japanese style means that during the day you live in the main room, which only has rice mats for a floor (leave your shoes at the door), no chairs (sit on the floor), and usually one main low table that sometimes has a charcoal stove (hibachi) under it for heat. Sparse but elegant. At night the maids bring out futons and this room then becomes the bedroom (sleep on the floor).

The hotel was within walking distance of everything I wanted to do.

First stop, one of the greatest of the almost unimaginable number of hot baths in Japan, the Tokyo Onsen.

Entering the Tokyo Onsen was like walking into another world. The entryway was beautifully appointed with hand rubbed wooden floors, lots of green plants, brilliant orchids, live bamboo plants, traditional Japanese semi-erotic drawings, and paintings and photos of Fuji. It was tranquil, serene, peaceful. Truly an oasis from the bustle of the Ginza outside.

We were immediately met by three girls wearing only panties and bras, and skimpy ones at that. My dad spoke quite a bit of Japanese by then so, after a few exchanges that my brother and I didn't understand, we seemed to be all set. The ladies directed us to a changing room were we
shed our western clothes and put on cotton kimonos, called yukata, which were used

at the time for lounging around the house and also as sleepwear.

We were ready.

Dad then informed us that while my brother and I were scheduled to be cycled through the main public facilities, he, for some reason, was going to have to go off with his lightly clad lady to a private room. We asked him why he wasn't staying with us, why did he need a private room?

His explanation didn't make any sense. When pressed for a better explanation he got very red in the face. We let it go. After all, we were teenagers and were focused on our own adventure. Years later it came to me that he might have had a different agenda. I'm sure some of you out
there are probably thinking that I'm kind of slow. I guess I am.

Entering the main hot bath rooms, our girls indicated that we should remove our yukatas and hang them up on hooks by the door. Remove our yukatas? We had nothing on underneath.

Oh my.

There we were. Two teenage boys standing naked in this huge open space being escorted by two very attractive girls wearing almost nothing and all around us were dozens more cute Japanese women all dressed, or rather, mostly undressed, the same. The scene was like some dream that I wished I'd had.

I realized that with this much naked female flesh we were going to have to be very careful to avoid embarrassing ourselves. Think of baseball, think of homework, think of chemistry. Wait, not chemistry.

We were in trouble.

Ahead of us was an enormous hot tub about 30 feet by 30 feet with ten Japanese businessmen in it, a girl hovering around each one, flirting, touching, serving drinks. There was a steam room, a dry sauna, a cold plunge, a wash room with eight marble slabs to lay on while being washed, private rooms with beds, four barber chairs, lounging chairs, easy chairs, a bar with another scantily clad girl tending it, and a strange room with a glass wall that faced out on this whole array that had bleachers in it. Did I mention that everywhere I looked there were cute, sexy girls wearing almost nothing?

Sensory overload.

The bleacher room was our first stop. The girls had us stand facing the glass wall, spread-eagled facing out into the large hot tub room. Standing behind us on the bleachers they began throwing large buckets of freezing cold water at us. It was kind of like they were the cheerleaders throwing water on the team in a private game with no fans. I never really understood what the purpose of this entire exercise was but, it took care of any possible disconcerting problems. In fact, we were quite shriveled up by the time they called a halt.

Next stop was the wash room. We each laid down on an eight-foot-long marble slab and the girls proceeded to wash us, carefully, softly, lovingly, hair, neck, arms, armpits, legs, feet, chest, back, buttocks, and then, well, then they came to that place.

My girl asked me something. I didn't understand. My brother's girl asked him something. He didn't understand. They made gestures that were suggestive, and we started to get the wrong idea. My brother finally figured out what they were trying to ask was; did we want to wash our private parts ourselves or should they do it for us.

Oh my heavens.

I knew that at 16 there was no way that I could avoid having an accident if I let my girl wash me. My brother and I looked at each other and at the same time turned to the girls and said "iie", which is NO in Japanese.

We opted for the self-wash.

After a final rinse the girls led us hand in hand to soak in the mammoth hot tub, marvelously clear considering the body load that must have been put through it each day. It was hot, it was really hot, but there were ten other guys in it, and we didn't want to look like complete babies, so we got in, trying not to scream. The girls lingered nearby, bringing us drinks, beer, wine, sake and fresh towels to dry the sweat off our faces. They were flirting, being cute and attentive which made us feel very important.

After about a half hour we were beckoned from the tub to sit in the barber chairs where we each got a haircut, pedicure and manicure. Then we alternated between the hot tub and cold plunge for another hour and regrettably our time was up.

I cannot tell you how many times I have wished that I had repeated this experience during my remaining time in Japan. What was I thinking? I lived a short train trip away. I could have gone any time again. I should have, could have, would have but, I didn't.

Dad appeared from where he had gone off to and settled up. I don't know what his private treatment cost, but I do remember that our time cost 1000 yen each, about three dollars. He seemed quite happy.

Our next stop was "the" spot in Tokyo for Kabuki theater.

The Nichigeki theater was ten stories tall at the time. It was a round building reminiscent of the Capitol Records building in Hollywood, California.

The bottom floor was Kabuki theater which is the traditional form of Japanese theater. All the actor's parts are played by men in layers and layers of troweled on makeup with marvelously improbable costumes. The acting is very stylized, almost stilted to a westerner's eyes. They speak in monotonous voices that, even if you could understand Japanese, would still be boring at 16, or even 60, and almost certainly if you are western.

This is not the level I wanted to go to.

The secret was, that as you went up higher in the building more clothes came off the actors, and, women were involved. We had been told that the very top floor was all women and full-frontal nudity.

That's the floor I wanted.

I begged, I pleaded with my dad. Please, please, please let's go to the tenth floor. You hate Kabuki, this is my birthday, mom won't care, I won't tell, the checks in the mail, I'll love you in the morning, come on dad! To this day I don't know why he said no. After all, our next stop was a strip club. I tried to explain that to him.

He bought tickets to Kabuki.

If you have never seen Kabuki and you get a chance to go, whatever else you do, leave yourself a way out. Make some excuse as to why you have to have an aisle seat or why you have to stand up in the back. Make up some excuse. Do not let yourself get trapped into a situation where getting up and forcing your way past a row of people would be impolite.

We had great seats right in the center of the fifth row. Yes, we were forced to suffer through the entire first act before we could mercifully make our exit. So much for full frontal nudity but, not to worry, the strip club was next.

Strip clubs. What's the deal here?

I must be missing a gene. I didn't understand this first one and I have never understood them since.

I'm not stupid. I like to look at a really nicely put together female body. I like beautifully formed breasts, slender arms, neat waists, dainty ankles, firm buttocks, great thighs, and that, well, that triangle part. I like a woman who is bright, witty, engaging, clever, artful, humorous, and fun to be with. A woman, who is dressed up, made up, confident and alive.

That's not what you get at a strip club. I mean the girls are usually tired, bored, and kind of unappetizing.

You get sweat, bad makeup, bad clothes, and bad company.

We walked into the strip club. Actually, it turned out it wasn't really a strip club but a gentleman's club. It was a place where lonely GI's and Japanese businessmen could enjoy female companionship, for a price. This wasn't what I expected. Well, I guess I don't know what I really expected. Maybe soft music, a beautiful entryway, a cute hostess to greet you, no pressure, soft lights, being escorted to a nice clean table, in an open room, tastefully clad but almost naked waitresses, and girls, lots of girls dancing close to you but not intruding on your space or embarrassing you.

A fantasy.

What we got was, well, what we got was... read the sentence above and just put in the opposite for every single item.

It was worse than Kabuki.

We came into this horrible place, no cute girl to greet us, bright lights, really smoky, and ugly ugly girls.

Okay, wait, I'm sorry (well, sort of sorry). I know it's not politically correct to call girls ugly but, right or wrong, men all have expectations or visions or probably prejudices that our parents or society have taught or convinced us is the female ideal.

Anyway, by my vision or prejudices, these girls were ugly.

I knew right away I didn't want to be there.

In fact, I sized up the situation and invented a move that has served me well for the last fifty years whenever I get into a situation like this. I put myself in the middle of the booth (next to a post works well also).

So, what's the big deal about that?

Well, it means when those skanky girls approached the booth, they couldn't sit next to me.

Sorry about that skanky comment but they were really not very attractive.

So, the picture was, one girl was seated next to my brother, one next to my dad, and the one assigned to me was across the table where she could talk to me but not reach me.

Then the strangest thing happened. This really fat, ugly, badly dressed, over made-up, sweaty girl who was seated next to my dad and put her hand in his crotch.

He lost his mind.

A minute before he had been a normal guy. Sitting there, conversing naturally, laughing, and joking with us. The next minute he had lost his ability to speak, his face was very red, he was breathing funny, and he was nodding his head up and down, agreeing to buy these girls champagne.

What happened here?

Well, I know what happened, and while it has happened to me on occasion it still is a mystery to me why the act, by a woman, of putting her hand in your crotch can cause otherwise normal sane rational beings to completely lose their minds.

My brother and I were embarrassed. The girl next to my brother tried the same maneuver which, of course, didn't work. He was fifteen and these women were at least twenty-five. Ancient by our standards. Being touched by, what was to our minds, a really old lady was not a turn-on. My girl was way across the table and thankfully couldn't get close to me.

I'd had enough in the first five minutes but, it took a half hour to pry my dad loose from there.

My three birthday wishes were complete and, while in some ways this whole trip wasn't what I had been expecting, in others it was more, and fifty years later it is still the birthday I remember the best.

Climbing Mount Fuji

"Worth-san, wake up!"

"Huh?"

I rolled over and opened my eyes. The concerned face of our head maid, Nobuko, was staring down at me. It was clear that she had been trying to wake me for quite some time.

"What's going on?" I asked sleepily.

"Bus go forty minute," she said.

"Bus?"

"Worth-san, today Fuji day," she explained.

That brought me out of my stupor. Today was Wednesday, the 26th of June, 1957, the date of our base's yearly scheduled trip to climb Mount Fuji. The Japanese had a saying that went something along the lines of being a fool if you never climbed Fuji once and twice a fool if you did it more than once. I had missed last year's trip because of being in the hospital with pleurisy. This was my final summer in Japan, and I didn't plan on missing the climb again.

"Baird, wake up or we're going to miss the bus," I shouted at my brother.

"What?"

"Baird, get dressed," I grumbled, pulling on my jeans. "The bus for Fuji leaves in forty minutes."

My brother dragged himself out of bed looking a bit shell-shocked. Actually, he was hung over. We had both been to the Teen Club the night before and he had consumed way too many glasses of Sun Tory Whiskey. I'd had to practically carry him home. The truth is I had consumed way too much myself, but I always seemed to handle it better.

"Is dad going to drive us?" he asked as he shrugged his shirt on.

"Baird, I know you're a lazy shit, but dad isn't getting out of bed for this," I said. "We are probably going to have to jog there unless we get lucky and hit the base bus."

"Worth, I can't. My head is..."

"Baird, I don't give a shit about your head," I interrupted. "I missed this trip last year because of that stupid pleurisy thing and there is no way I'm missing this one."

"But..."

"Fuck you, Baird," I said angrily. "Stay here then."

I grabbed my backpack and headed for the door.

"Wait," Baird pleaded. "I'm coming."

Baird was a year younger, but we were really close and did almost everything together. I really didn't want to leave him, but I was going. This was my final summer in Japan. Dad was due to be rotated stateside at the end of the next school year and I would never get another chance. I walked out.

He caught up to me, huffing and puffing and complaining about his head and lack of sleep, before I got down the hill. We could see the base shuttle bus in the cul-de-sac and started running. The door had closed, and it was just starting to move when we swooped down and began beating a tattoo on the sides, screaming 'chotto matte' ('wait a minute') at the Japanese driver. We scared the hell out of him. He slammed on the brakes, opened the door and we piled in.

"Worth," Baird began again, "my head hurts and I really need..."

"Baird," I said, stopping him in mid-sentence, "you can sleep on the bus all the way there."

"Why are we doing this anyway, Worth?" my brother asked.

"Look, I told you don't have to..."

"No, I mean why are we going, really?" he interrupted.

I looked at him. I didn't have a good answer. Why **was** I going? Because it was there? Because I could? Because I was bored? Because I was trying to prove myself? Maybe. At least I would be able to say that I was one of the few people who had been on the top of Mount Fuji as the sun came up.

"Don't really know, bud," I said. "I just want to."

He wasn't listening. I had taken too long to answer, and he was fast asleep. I let him nap until the bus reached the meeting point at the Officer's Club and then gently shook him.

"Time to go, bud," I said softly.

"Huh?"

I ignored him, picked up my backpack and stepped off the bus. He stumbled out behind me. The motor pool bus that would take us to Fuji was waiting as were twenty or so of my closest friends.

It might seem strange that I had so many 'close' friends, but we were strangers in a strange land. Unlike normal kids our age, that is to say stateside kids, we bonded. There were only about thirty of us high school students on the base and we did everything together. We spent almost two hours a day riding the bus to school in winter and all our summers together at the pool. There was always something going on at the Teen Club and every weekend was one long party. We played together, partied together, took trips together and fell in and out of love together.

I looked around. My best friend Bert, his brother Ken and the goofy but lovable Billy Woodall were standing at the back of the bus, eyeing the girls. Bert and I hadn't gotten along at all when we first met but one day the Sergeant who ran the Teen Club activities program changed all that. Sergeant Strickler put us in a boxing ring to duke it out. In three rounds Bert had managed to destroy me. I was bleeding from the mouth and nose and staggering around in a daze when the 'Sarge' stepped in and stopped the fight. Funny thing was we had been best buds ever since.

"Bert, I thought you weren't going," I said.

"Yeah, I wasn't."

"What changed your mind?" I asked.

"Might as well."

"Might as well?" I laughed.

"Yeah, better than staying here, I guess."

"Uh huh," I nodded. "Because...?"

"So many of the group are going the Club will be dead tonight," he said.

"I see. So, you're going because the Club will be dead," I said, shaking my head.

"Yeah."

"Are you going to try for sunrise?"

"Might as well," he said grudgingly.

"And your brother?" I asked, pointing at Ken.

"He's like your brother," Bert chuckled. "He always wants to do whatever I'm doing because he's afraid he's going to miss something."

I laughed and looked around at the rest of the group. Actually, I looked to see which girls had decided to come. Two that I really liked and wanted to date were there. Fumiko, whose dad was a second generation Japanese-American and who had been on base the longest of any of us, was standing and talking to her current boyfriend John. I had tried for two years to date her with no luck. We were friends but that was as far as it went.

Kitty, who was a recent arrival, was standing by herself. I waved and she waved back but didn't walk over. Kitty had arrived at almost the end of this past school year. She had been totally lost and alone her first day. She had been crying and her face was closed down as she stepped on the bus for our daily one plus hour ride into Tokyo. In truth it was never easy for any of us to change schools and leave our friends and this move had been particularly hard on her as she had been desperately in love with a boy she had to leave.

For once in my life I had acted on an impulse and, as she passed my seat, I stood up and invited her to sit down. We hit it off and went steady for about three weeks before the football jocks discovered her, and I was left on the outside looking into the candy store with my nose pressed up against the window. I looked at her now with longing, but I was wasting my time.

"All right boys and girls," a voice said. "It's time to mount up."

Sergeant Strickler was standing at the door to the bus. The bravest of us called him 'Sarge' but most of the kids addressed him as 'Sergeant Strickler'. I was one of the braver ones.

"Hey Sarge," I said. "How'd you get this duty?"

"Well if it isn't Mister 'Wild Red Berry'," he observed. "Going to climb today?"

"God damn it, Sarge!" I blurted.

"Sorry, boy," he said. "But I like that persona you picked for the wrestling team."

"Sarge," I pleaded, "my friends are here."

"Yeah, I see them," he chuckled. "Isn't that 'The Czech' and 'Bruiser' and 'The Executioner' standing over there?"

He had a point. Half of my friends were on the team he had convinced us to start. He told us that wrestling was a way to learn some judo moves and falls and have fun putting on shows at the base clubs. All we had done up to now was practice.

"I got you boys a gig," he continued.

"What?"

"You are the opening act at the Yakota Officer's Club in two weeks," he explained.

"The opening act?" I said dumbly.

"Yeah, they wanted a warm-up act before the B-girls came on," he laughed. "They are going to pay us twenty-five bucks. Got your costume done yet?"

"No, sir," I said. "But I will."

"No need to call me sir, boy, I work for a living," he snapped. "Get on the bus."

I climbed on and sat down. I thought about the wrestling team. Sarge had assured us that Professional Wrestling was the hot new entertainment in New Orleans where he had just been stationed. Grown men, dressed in outlandish costumes, throwing each other around a ring. It had captured our imagination. We were having a lot of fun pretending to hurt each other. Wow, our first match! I just hoped that everyone else thought it was as fun to watch. The bus started and I tried to concentrate on the challenge ahead instead of worrying about how I was going to get all the items that I needed for my costume in just two weeks.

There are four main routes up Mount Fuji, located roughly on the North, South, East and West faces with ten 'stations' or rest stops on each route. A few true purists start at the base of the mountain at station one and climb from there. The vast majority of people take the easy way and start from about halfway up at one of the four 'fifth stations' that are on each route. By far the most popular route begins from the North side at the Kawaguchiko 5th station which is where we climbed out of the bus about three hours later.

"Wow, look at this place, Worth," my brother said. "It looks like a tourist trap."

It looked like a tourist trap because it was. There were dozens of stores all selling exactly the same stuff: Miniature Fujis, Fuji key chains, Fuji postcards, Fuji maps, Fuji and Japanese flags, hundreds of different garish pictures and paintings of Fuji and... climbing sticks. We didn't need the other stuff, but we needed climbing sticks.

The sticks weren't really to climb with, although they did help. Mostly they became the keepsake and proof that you had really climbed. They are a six-foot-long hexagonal shaft of some really lightweight but strong wood on which you had each station brand a stamp. The hardest one to get was the 'Sunrise' stamp which you could only get for about a half an hour after the sun came up and only on the top.

"How much? Stick?" I asked the mama-san minding the store we went into.

She held up ten fingers and blinked them twice saying, "San ju."

Thirty yen. At the going exchange rate of three hundred sixty-five yen to the dollar that was... too little to even think about. I picked up two sticks and handed her sixty yen.

"Stampu" I mimed, pretending to press a stamp on my shaft.

"Hai," she responded, taking both sticks and stepping to a small hibachi with a branding iron.

When she was finished, she handed them back.

"Ni ju, dozo," she said.

"What'd she say?" my brother asked.

"Twenty yen, bud," I answered, "less than a dime."

"Did dad give you money?" he asked.

"It's a little late to be thinking about that now, isn't it?" I chuckled.

"I guess."

"Yeah, he did," I said. "He gave me three thousand yen. He told me there was no way we'd spend it all."

We walked outside and looked for our group. Most of the others had also purchased sticks and were milling next to the start of the trail. I looked around to find 'Sarge'. He had climbed back in the bus and shut the door. I walked over, rapped on the door and he cranked it open.

"What's going on, Sarge?" I asked. "Aren't you going with us?"

"And slog my way up that hill?" he laughed.

"Yes."

"Son, I've slogged my way up plenty of hills during my time," he explained. "I think I'll just sit this one out."

"You mean you're going to wait here until noon tomorrow?" I asked incredulously.

"Not exactly."

"What are you going to do then?" I asked.

"Got other plans, son," he said with a twinkle in his eye.

"Other plans?" I asked stupidly.

"Going to find me a mama-san for the night," he explained.

"A mama-san?"

A vision of the old woman who had just sold me climbing sticks flitted through my mind.

"I'm going to a strip club, son, and find me a girl."

"Oh."

"Tomorrow noon, boy," he said and closed the door.

I knew about Japanese strip clubs. Every base had dozens just outside. In fact, I had talked my dad into taking me to one in Tokyo on my sixteenth birthday. I didn't get the attraction but then the women had all been old and somewhat overweight. My dad had loved it. The biggest lesson of that night was when a fat ugly girl had seated herself beside him and put her hand on his leg. He was ready to agree to anything she wanted. I don't think the sight of my dad losing his mind like that was one I ever wanted to see again. I didn't like it. I pretended to feel sick so we could go back to the hotel.

"They're leaving, Worth," my brother whined, bring me back from my reverie.

I looked at the trailhead and most of the group was already strung out in a line walking up.

"Okay, bud, let's go," I said, and we hustled to catch them.

The first part of the trail remained below the tree line. Tall pine trees shaded us from the fierce summer sun and the trail wasn't steep at all. Everyone was in great spirits. I looked for Kitty, but I saw that she had already hooked up with Smokey, who happened to be my wrestling partner. Smokey stood about six foot three and packed two hundred forty pounds of pure muscle. At six foot and only one fifty myself it always made me chuckle that in our matches I got to almost win. Actually, I got to do a whole bunch of nasty and illegal things to him and then cheat to almost win. Before he took over and pinned me.

I'm sure the audience was going to have to suspend a lot of belief to swallow that.

The way Kitty was leaning into him forced him to sling an arm around her shoulder to keep them both straight. I was jealous. I consoled myself with the fact that Kitty had been my girlfriend once for two weeks or so and concentrated on hiking up the trail.

***

The sixth station is well above the tree line and we were hot and dusty by the time we got there. I bought my brother and

I a coke to share and then we queued up at the hibachi for our stamp. After parting with another twenty yen we walked over to where some of the others were resting. Billy Woodall wasn't looking all that great.

"Hey, Billy, what's up?" I asked.

"This is really hard."

"Billy," I chided, "we're only at a little over 8000 feet. The top is above twelve and it gets steeper."

"I don't think I can do this," he complained.

"Want me to walk with you?" I asked.

"Can't I just stay here?"

"Sure, Billy, but..."

"But what?"

"Why not try?" I asked. "It's early. You can take it easy."

"Okay," he grumbled struggling to his feet.

The trail out of station six got a lot steeper with more rocks and plenty of switchbacks. Baird and I stayed back with Billy while most of the rest out climbed us and were gone. As we got farther up the mountain the view was breathtaking! It was a beautiful clear day and you could see Sagami bay, which led into Tokyo bay and you could even get a glimpse of Tokyo. Billy was in a lot distress when we arrived at what we assumed was station seven at least an hour behind the others. I sat him down at a table, gathered our sticks and approached the papa-san standing by the hibachi.

"Shichi?" I asked, using the Japanese word for seven.

"Hai" he replied, bowing.

"This ain't seven, fella," a voice said behind me.

I turned. A twenty something GI was sitting at the table next to Baird and Billy drinking a Nehi orange soda.

"It's not?"

"No, this is a fake seven," he said. "This guy is just an entrepreneur who's looking to make a buck from tourists."

"A fake seven?"

"Yeah, there are lots of fake stations," he explained. "You want to be sure that you just get your stamps from the official stations."

I thought about that.

"Why?"

"Because...well...they're fake," he stuttered.

"I don't care," I said.

"Huh?"

"What difference does it make? The stamps are cool and who's going to know anyway?" I joked. "Do they have climbing stick police?"

"I just thought you'd like to know, kid," he said angrily.

"Hey thanks," I said contritely. "I appreciate it."

"Sure, kid."

I turned back to pay the papa-san when he spoke again.

"Hey, kid, are you going for the summit?"

I looked back at him.

"Uh huh."

"You planning on sunrise?" he asked.

"Uh huh."

"You planning on stopping to rest?" he asked.

"We thought we'd stop at station eight until about two in the morning," I explained. "That's what we've been told is a good way to do it."

"It is but..."

"But...?"

"It's getting late, kid," he said. "You ain't going to make eight before dark."

"Oh."

"I'm just telling you that the trail gets a lot steeper and people have died so be careful."

"Hey, thanks," I said sincerely.

"Sure, kid, good luck."

I turned to Billy and Baird.

"Let's go guys, we're late," I said.

"I can't," Billy whined. "My head hurts and...'

"Billy," I interrupted, "I want to get there by sunrise."

"I know, Worth, but I'm holding you guys back and I'm really feeling sick."

"One more station?" I suggested.

"I don't think I can."

"Okay, Billy," I said. "Rest here and we'll pick you up on the way down. Or else just start down in the morning and meet us in the parking lot."

"Thanks, Worth," he said.

"Be careful, Billy," I replied, shrugging my backpack on. "See you tomorrow."

"Can I stay here too?" my brother asked.

"No."

"Why not?"

"Get your pack, we're going to see sunrise from the top."

***

We arrived at the real station eight well after dark. Along the way we did find the real seventh station and a bunch of other stations that claimed they were sevens and eights. Our sticks were festooned with stamps. The trail was hard and steep and covered with rocks and crosses.

We had gone by more crosses where people had died than I cared to remember. Another climber told us that most people died on the way down when they were not being careful. They died when they were exalted and exhausted from the climb and got going down too fast and went over the edge.

We were tired but still in good spirits and excited. We would be resting here until about two in the morning which would allow us two hours to climb the final 1500 vertical feet to the summit.

The only light in the eighth station was the soft glow from the hibachi in the entrance and a few candles around the room. The papa-san was happy to see us as only five other people had stopped, and he needed the business. None of the people resting there were our friends. In fact, all of them were Japanese. I wondered how we had missed all the rest of our group on the only trail on this side of the mountain. I decided that perhaps they had gone further up.

"I'm thirsty," my brother said.

"Want a coke?"

"Can we get some Sun Tory?" he asked.

"Didn't you have enough last night?"

"This is a special case," he said.

"You always say that," I smiled.

"Do they have it?"

"I can ask," I laughed.

I turned to the papa-san.

"Sun Tory ka?"

"iie," he said, shaking his head.

"Beeru ka?" I asked.

"iie."

"Dan, he says they don't have any Sun Tory or beer."

"Mark, I need something to drink," Dan whined, "what about sake?"

"Sake ka?" I asked.

"Hai!"

He stepped into an alcove and brought back a large bottle of sake that he poured into smaller serving containers. He put those in front of us along with two sake cups. We each poured a cup and sat back.

"Are you hungry, Dan?" I asked.

"I don't know," he replied, "what do they have?"

"Probably rice."

"I'm sick of rice," he complained.

"They might have tofu," I said.

He glared at me, shook his head and poured himself another cup of sake. I looked around the grubby hut and marveled over the fact that I was sitting on the side of a mountain half way around the world from my home, drinking sake. I poured more sake and stretched out on the futons to wait for the final ascent.

* * *

I must have been much wearier that I realized because the next thing I remember is the papa-san shaking me awake. I looked at my watch. It was ten past two and the hut was empty except for my brother who was snoring.

"Time to go, Baird," I shouted.

He snapped his head up and glared at me.

"You know sometimes I get really sick of your harebrained schemes," he said angrily.

"You always come along," I quipped.

"That's because I'm afraid I might miss something," he admitted.

"You might," I said.

"I get sick of it," he said.

"Do you?"

"Yes, like that time when you talked me into going to the Chiba peninsula for the weekend," he said.

"What was wrong with that?" I asked.

"Don't you remember that papa-san who almost killed us in the hot tub?" he asked.

"Killed us?"

"Remember how hot the tub was and he just stepped in and then we had to get the rest of the way in to prove that we weren't wussys and..."

"It wasn't that hot," I said shaking my head.

"It wasn't that hot?" he said incredulously. "It took you fifteen minutes just to get in up to your thighs."

"I wasn't in any hurry," I said.

"Anyway, then that old Japanese guy steps in and sits down like its nothing."

"They're built differently than we are, and they're used to it," I said.

"I thought I was going to be disfigured for life," he complained.

"You were fine."

"And then you insisted that we go out in those six-foot waves, remember?"

"That was fun," I said. "It was...really exciting."

"I almost drowned."

"I saved you," I said mildly.

"Worth, I was in trouble," he said angrily.

"I saved you, bud," I repeated.

"I wouldn't have to have been saved in the first place if you didn't keep dragging me along," he grumbled.

"Want to stay here?" I asked. "I'll pick you up on the way down."

"Fuck you."

***

The final fifteen hundred feet of vertical were hell. It was dark and we hadn't brought but one flashlight. The trail was rocky and so steep in places we were almost crawling. We weren't used to the altitude, so we had to stop every minute to catch our breath.   We stopped at station nine long enough to get a stamp and then went back to our upward trudge.

We did the last five hundred feet by just taking five steps at a time and then resting a minute and then five more steps. I had to carry Baird's pack the last two hundred feet, or he would have never made it. We collapsed at the summit. Well, we collapsed at the rim but from there it was an easy walk to the highest point.

"We...made... it, bud," I panted.

"I don't...know why...I let you...talk me into this shit," he replied.

"We made it, Baird," I effused. "Do you realize what an exclusive club we belong to?"

"Exclusive club?"

"Baird, do you know how many people there are in the world?" I asked.

"Um...a lot?"

"Right," I said, "a lot, and do you know how many have been on the top of this mountain?"

"Uh...not many?" he said.

"Not many at all and of those how many have been here at four in the morning?" I asked.

"Wow," he said, finally getting the concept. "That is really cool."

"Cool indeed, brother," I agreed, "now let's get over to the sunrise hut and wait."

The actual highest point on the summit was on the other side of the crater from where we were. It took almost a half an hour to walk over. As we did it got lighter and lighter. I looked around and only about fifty people had actually made the summit. I thought of all the hopefuls we had seen at the bottom and all the people we had passed on the way up. Not one of my friends had made it.

Then it happened. Like magic the sun peeked out of the horizon. Every face turned to it and not a person moved.

Looking down the mountain trail on this side I could see dozens of hopefuls strung out down the slope who hadn't quite made the summit. Each of them was silent also and turned to the sun.

That silence lasted until the other side of the sun broke the horizon and then the spell was over. We queued up to get our stamp.

I had just turned from paying the man for my stamp when I saw her. She was sitting on a bench about twenty feet away. 'She' was an American girl wearing short shorts, a short sleeve blouse and flimsy sandals. I was incredulous and I was smitten. I walked over and sat down.

"Hi," I said carefully.

She looked at me shyly.

"Hi."

"Did you climb like that?" I asked stupidly.

"Like what?"

"Dressed like that?"

"Yeah."

"Wow! All the way up here in those sandals?" I gushed.

"Uh huh."

"What's your name?"

"Trixie," she replied. "What's yours?"

"I'm Worth and that's my little brother Baird," I answered, pointing over to where he was standing. "Where are you from?"

"Yamagata."

"Yamagata? That's way to the north, right?" I asked.

"Yeah, its seven hours by train," she said. "We came down two days ago just to climb."

"We?" I pressed.

"My parents and my brother," she explained.

I looked around but I didn't see any other Americans. I looked back at her.

"Where are they?"

She shrugged and replied, "I'm not sure. I left them back at station seven about midnight and just kept climbing.'

"Are you cold?" I asked moving closer and putting my arm around her.

"A little," she said, snuggling into me.

I put my other arm around her and looked down at her. She turned her head, looked up and we kissed. To this day I can remember that kiss. I've had three in my life like that one. It was one of those take the top of your head off, feel like you are passing out, heart stopping, toe curling kind of kisses that went on and on.

"My god," I choked out when we broke.

"Mmmm," she purred.

I leaned in again. I wanted another one of those. We tuned the world out.

"Hey, Worth," my brother interrupted. "Don't we have to go down soon?"

I looked daggers at him.

"No," I said testily, "and...can't you see I'm busy?"

I turned to Trixie. She was looking up at me with a dazed expression. Clearly, she felt the same as I did.

"Do you have a boyfriend?" I asked.

"No," she whispered.

"Do you...uh...want to go...steady?" I stammered.

"Yes," she said and turned her face up for another kiss.

"Worth, we are going to miss the bus," my brother said behind me.

"God damn it," I shouted. "It's only about six and we don't have to be at the parking lot until noon!"

"I just thought we should get going is all," he said.

"Go without me," I snapped.

"No, I can wait."

He had managed to ruin the moment. We got up hand in hand like the new lovers we were.

"What time do you have to meet your parents," I asked.

"Noon in the parking lot at station five," she answered.

"Which station five?"

"Kawaguchiko."

"Me too," I said. "We can go down together then."

"Okay."

"Want to walk down into the crater?" I asked.

"I'd like that."

"Baird, Trixie and I are going to walk down into the crater. Why don't you stay here?" I asked pointedly. "We'll be back in about an hour and start down then."

He looked at me with a hurt expression, but he finally got the message. He sat down on the bench.

"Come on, Trixie,' I said tenderly. "Let's check this out."

We spent an hour in the crater, most of the time kissing. She let me run my hands up her blouse and feel her breasts through her bra. I had never touched a girl there before and once my hands were there, I didn't know what to do so I just squeezed a little. She seemed to like it.

I was sorry when it was time to go because I could have stayed there and kissed her forever. Baird was still sitting on the bench when we got back. He looked sullen.

"Ready?" I asked.

"I could see you guys you know," he said testily.

"So?"

"So, I was kind of bored sitting here while you guys were making out, that's what," he whined.

"Sorry, bud."

"Sure."

We made our way back across the crater to the Kawaguchiko trail and started down. Surprisingly it was almost as hard as coming up. We were using different muscles and my legs were aching by the time we got to the ninth station. I could see how people died. It was easy to get going too fast and very hard to stop yourself once you had momentum going. We scared ourselves more than once.

Just past the eighth station, at a steep switchback, we crossed a lava slide. You could see that the lava slide paralleled the route down all the way to the tree line. It looked inviting but we had been warned that they were incredibly dangerous and to never get on one. I had been holding Trixie's hand in the shallower stretches, but it was steep on this section and she was just ahead of me with Baird behind me as we stopped to look at the view.

Then, before I could react, Trixie stepped onto the lava slide and started running down it, whooping and hollering. She was a hundred feet below us and still moving when I snapped out of my stupor and followed. I heard my brother curse, looked back and he was on the slide also.

It was crazy and scary but actually way easier than the trail. We did the first two thousand feet of vertical in about thirty minutes. Trixie lost her sandals in the first five hundred feet and the lava sliced her feet badly. I looked for some way to get back on the trail, but we were committed. We stopped and I gave her my socks and tore my shirt into two large pieces that we used to bind her feet to protect them. It helped but she could barely walk by the time we rejoined the trail. We limped along together down the last two thousand feet and I had to carry her for the final half mile. We collapsed at the fifth station around ten in the morning. Billy was there, having descended at first light. We got green tea and waited for the bus, her parents and my friends. They started trickling in, each with a different story. Bert came in about an hour after us.

"Bert, what happened to you guys?" I asked.

"We went the wrong way around station eight and ended up on the Fujinomiya trail," he said. "We got to the summit about seven."

"Really? Wow, we just missed each other," I said. "That's just when we left."

"Bummer."

"Did you get your stamp?" I asked.

"They gave me a 'Top' stamp but said it was too late for the sunrise one," he said glumly.

"Well you made it just the same," I said encouragingly.

"Yeah."

I could see him eyeing Trixie. I didn't like it. He was always too chummy with my girlfriends. I decided to head him off.

"Hey, Bert," I said. "This is Trixie. We're going steady."

I could see the change in his eyes. Girls were fair game, but you didn't mess with a guy's 'steady'.

"Hi, Trix," he said, but his mind was already elsewhere.

Kitty and Smokey got back at eleven. They had some story that didn't make sense about getting lost and having to spend the night somewhere. I was jealous. Trixie noticed and put her hand on my arm. I turned to her and forgot about them.

Her parents and brother showed up the same time Sergeant Strickler did. It hadn't hit me until then, but I was going one direction and Trixie another. She looked at me with a stricken, lost look in her eyes which I'm sure mirrored mine.

"I guess this is it, huh?" she said.

"Can't we get together?" I asked.

"How?"

"I don't know. Don't you ever get down here?"

"No."

"Would your parents let me visit?" I asked.

"Visit?"

"Yeah. Up there where you guys live," I said.

"Worth..."

"I could come next weekend," I said. "I can take the train."

"By yourself?"

"Trixie, this is Japan. I travel all the time by myself."

"Really?"

"Ask your parents if I can come."

She turned and got their attention.

"Mom," she asked, "would it be okay if Worth came and visited next weekend?"

Mom looked at me, but her eyes were glazed over. I'm sure she was thinking that they lived seven hours away and saying yes was not a big deal because that 'boy' would never show. I smiled inwardly but kept my face clam.

"Sure, honey," she said, "we'd love to have him."

I waited until both of them were distracted, then leaned over and kissed her lightly on the lips.

"See you next weekend," I whispered.

"Really?"

"Do you want me to come?" I asked.

"Yes."

"I'll be there."

Note 1: Most of this is a true story. I did climb Fuji, I did meet that girl, we did share an incredible kiss, she did run down the lava slide forcing us to follow, but unfortunately even though I could have gone to see her I was fifteen years old with the attention span of a gnat.

Note 2: I went back to Japan on the fiftieth anniversary of this climb. I brought a friend who was definitely a Billy Woodall. I pushed him to the eighth station but he couldn't make it further and I was unwilling to leave him, so I saw sunrise from the eighth station.

Note 3: While the lava slides were considered dangerous in 1957 by the time I climbed again in 2007 the Japanese had figured out that it was a much safer path down. Deaths have greatly diminished on Mount Fuji.

Sayonara

I know you know this but Sayonara means goodbye in Japanese.

When you think about it, I guess it's not surprising that we returned home on the same ship that we came over on, the General Edwin D. Patrick. After all the ships job, in those days, was to ferry dependents and hard goods back and forth between San Francisco and Yokohama. The trip took a week each way, so it was in Yokohama every two weeks.

We departed Yokohama, in mid-summer of 1958, with the usual paper streamers and band. All our maids were standing on the pier, waving and crying, to watch us go   We got the same staterooms, the same room steward, and the same mess steward. It was like coming home. My
brother and I knew that ship from stem to stern.

Dad was the highest-ranking traveler and thus mom was the highest-ranking wife so they were completely occupied organizing all kinds of events to fill up the days, which left my brother and I to further explore the ship.

It was a game to see how far we could get into the ship without being discovered. We thought we had really explored the first time but on this voyage, we set goals. We got back to the bow on the lowest deck where we had been to become "Shellbacks" three years before. We got to the bridge,
but we had to ask a crew member as it was always manned. We got to watch the crew throw garbage off the stern (which the sharks following the ship loved). It passed the time.

Two days from San Francisco we stopped for a day in Honolulu. Keeping with our status as semi-adults, dad let us go off on our own.

"Just be back on the ship before four", he said, "because we sail at five."

Off we went into the island wonderland that was 50's Oahu. Oh my! Warm, blue sky, great temperature, lots of things to see and do. We only had about six hours, so we took a cab right away to a beach that even as teenagers we had heard about. We went directly to Waikiki, with its beautiful old hotels, trucked in sand, view of Diamond Head, tanned bikini clad, well 50's bikini clad, wahines, and gigolos.

Oh yes, the gigolos of Wakiki. Bronzed, young, well-built Hawaiian men, not much older than we were, whose only job in life was to cater to women, of any age, for a price. Who they were and what they were doing was obvious even to us. They hung out in groups on the beach and seemed to have a sixth sense about their prey, sometimes pairs of women and sometimes a woman walking the beach alone. Always an offer to ride a long board or show them some coral in the water. The women seemed to enjoy the attention even if they didn't buy into the ride.

Think about this, you are a forty-year-old woman with two kids, whose husband doesn't pay attention to you anymore, maybe a few pounds heavier than you should be, maybe a few more wrinkles here and there and, that little waddle under your chin has been bothering you a lot lately, and here comes a buff, 20 year old, cute, easy going, artful guy who pays attention to you. No, more than pays attention, really listens, flirts, is considerate, caring, holds the door (well perhaps there weren't any doors on the beach), caresses you, gives you weapons-grade looks, has a sense of humor, knows how to kiss, actually, really knows how to kiss, how to give great massages... I could go on and on, but I think you get the idea, a short-term fantasy without the mortgage. I think that those guys invented Vegas's latest slogan because in the 50's what happened with gigolos stayed with gigolos.

We had an incredible day. We spent the day watching the girls and the waves, walking the beach and lying on it, playing in the waves and, by parting with some of our cash, we each took a quick ride on a long board with a gigolo type who must have been having a slow day.

At the end of the day I bought some surf pants, which were all the rage. These pants were kind of long shorts similar to the style of swimming trunks kids, and adults too, I guess, wear today. When they got wet, they clung to you, sopping wet, uncomfortable, irritating, and miserable to wear. I wore them one time before I went back to (gasp) "speedos". I will take comfort over fashion any day.

We got back to the pier and everyone, absolutely everyone was aboard the ship. The band was standing, waiting to play, the hula girls were milling around waiting to dance, the leis had all been handed out and the crew was standing by waiting to pull the gangplank. My dad and the Captain were standing at the end of the gangplank and the Captain was mad as hell but, hey, we were immature, juvenile, semi-adults so it rolled right off us.

As the ship moved away from the pier, I threw my orchid lei into the scummy waters like I had been told. "If you throw your lei into the waters, you will return to Hawaii", was the mantra. It must have worked because I have been back since, but all I remember of that departure was watching my lei, floating there in those oily waters, and thinking, 'what a terrible waste of orchids'.

Well, if you've read this book from the beginning you know what happened next. That's right, LIFEBOAT DRILL, where we all got to stand in the late afternoon sun and humidity waiting for those inconsiderate, uncaring brain-dead people who never show up for those drills.

The Golden Gate, two days later, was a beautiful sight but the end of a time that I have remembered off and on all my life. I have used snippets of the experiences, memories, and just general nonsense and crazy times that I had there, to regale friends and family for fifty years.

The life lessons and the independence we learned changed our lives and shaped our destinies. My brother went on to a successful career in industry, eventually retiring as the CEO of a 3.5billion dollar company.

And I, well, I got a book out of the whole deal.

end

Made in the USA
Monee, IL
16 February 2022